BREATHLESS 3

IN LOVE WITH AN ALPHA BILLIONAIRE

By Shani Greene-Dowdell

Published by Nayberry Publications (2015)
Opelika, Alabama, 36801, USA

Designed by Nayberry Publications

Ebook Published by David Weaver Presents
Paperback Published by Nayberry Publications

Printed in the United States of America

PUBLISHER'S NOTE

In the Name of Love…

<u>Acknowledgements</u>

To the husband, thanks for your tough love and support.

To Kim, Athena and Anthony, thanks for listening to my story plot ideas and giving me pointers.

To Theresa, I couldn't have finished this without you pushing me and sending ideas.

To David Weaver, thanks again for the collaboration.

To you, reading this book right now, thank you wholeheartedly. I hope you enjoy the finale.

Blessings,
Shani

Also by Shani Greene-Dowdell

Breathless: In Love With An Alpha Billionaire

Breathless 2: In Love With An Alpha Billionaire

Secrets of a Kept Woman 1

Secrets of a Kept Woman 2

Secrets of a Kept Woman 3: You Can't Help Who You Love

The Most Wonderful Time of the Year

Savor: The Longest Night Anthology

Mocha Chocolate 1-2 Anthology

Prologue

Jacob

Recap

After seeing Destiny and Ms. Clara onto their flight to Atlanta, I felt the need to do something that would take my mind off the shocking events that occurred at dinner. I dressed in a pair of shorts, tee and running shoes and went for a run on the trail surrounding my parents' property. My feet hit the pavement in earnest as I thought about Mom inviting Justine to have dinner with us. It was a spit in the face to both me and the woman I loved. I had never felt so disrespected by my mother in all my life. All hope of the two most important women in my life having an amicable relationship was squashed after that stunt.

But as it turned out, being spiteful towards Destiny was the least of Mom's worries. After Ms. Clara's spirited slap to my father's jaw and him rushing off behind her for a hug, we found out Ms. Clara had been the long, lost love of my father's life. And their past relationship wasn't nearly as potent as the way they peered into each other's eyes upon reconnecting. Dad looked at her as if all the years they were apart simply vanished.

When Ms. Clara rounded the dining room table and stood in front of Dad, I could see him transport back to 1975. He looked like a young chap who'd just spotted his first love. It was remarkable to watch and a train wreck at the same time.

As I finished off my third mile and headed toward the house, I felt a little better, but I still had so much tension in my body. The last thing Destiny and I needed was another layer of stress added to our relationship. My father admitting to loving her mother all the years he was supposed to be loving my mother was definitely an added stress.

Everything I considered the norm for my family had been shattered in a matter of seconds. Don't get me wrong, I always wanted more out of a relationship than what my parents shared. I desired a deeper connection with the woman I loved. As I thought back to when I was a young boy, I remembered that Mom and Dad never displayed a great level of passion for one another.

After observing my parent's lackluster bond, I knew Justine and I would be passing lovers. She and I had met at a crossroad, when we both needed someone. However, the initial protective feelings soon passed for me and I was bound and determined not to spend my life tied to a woman I didn't love. I had just hoped my parents, in their own way, had a stronger bond that couldn't be broken.

I entered the kitchen and got a bottle of Aquadeco out the fridge. I tossed back the cool liquid as I thought about how passionately in love I was with Destiny. I smiled as I thought of how I was consumed with fire, whenever I was with her. We had the type of love I always wanted. The ember that ignited when I met her outside of Tazi's eatery in Atlanta was now an all-consuming flame. No amount of water would ever be able to put it out. No weapons formed against us would ever be able to change my love for the woman my heart belonged to for all of eternity.

The big smile on my face was replaced with a frown as I looked at the stairwell leading to Mom's bedroom. I had to address Mom sooner rather than later. It was past time we had yet another talk about the bullshit she kept pulling with Justine. I couldn't understand why she kept pulling for Justine when that was not who I wanted. Either way, I needed to get her to understand this was her final chance to pick a side.

I tossed the empty bottle in the trash and took the winding stairs to Mom's room. I creaked open her door and peeked in. Normally, at this hour, she would be up writing out her list of things to do the next day, but she was lying in the dark with her head buried underneath her covers when I entered the room.

"Mom, are you awake?"

She didn't answer, but her quivers let me know she was awake. Her covers rose and fell in rapid motion showing her distress over the evening.

"Mom, we need to talk." Upon hearing my voice, her cry filled the room with solemnness. "Mom, I'm pissed that you would invite Destiny to dinner and then have Justine there. I told Destiny you were ready to accept her and then you pull this? Were you trying to make me look like a fool this whole time?"

Again, she didn't say anything. She just pulled the covers tighter and sobbed her pain. It was obvious she needed some time to sort out her feelings, but after the way she treated Destiny I didn't care. It was mighty convenient for her to be in her feelings after causing my fiancé grief.

The only thing stopping me from digging in deeper was that she was dealing with Dad's reunion with Ms. Clara. But she needed to spend an equal amount of time contemplating what she'd done to our relationship. We were on the verge of a very strained relationship as mother and son.

"It's pretty damn convenient for you to lay here and act like a victim, Mom. What you put out in this world is what you get back," I said as her sobs became louder. "You know what, fuck this! I'm going to drop it for tonight, but we are going to talk tomorrow," I assured her, as I closed the door behind me. I hoped by morning the woman who was brave enough to stand by Justine's side in the courtroom in Atlanta and was conniving enough to invite her to dinner last night would show up. I didn't want to talk to the weak and feeble woman lying in that bed tonight.

Next, I headed to Dad's study. When I entered, he too was sitting in darkness, except for a small lamp burning on his desk.

"Hi Son," he said, as I sat in the plush burgundy chaise in front of his desk.

"Do you care to explain what just happened?" I asked.

There was weariness in his eyes as he looked up at me. He picked up a crystal glass filled with brown liquor and took a healthy gulp before replying to my question. "You're a smart man, trusted to head a billion-dollar company. Do you really need an explanation of what happened, Jacob?"

"No, I understand what happened. The fact that you and Ms. Clara had a thing for each other is clear. I just want you to tell me where your mind is right now. I want to hear from the horse's mouth why our family is about to go belly up."

"How do you feel about Destiny?" he asked, dropping his pen on his desk.

"You're answering my question with a question."

"Yes."

"Alright, I love her," I answered.

"Is that all you can say about the woman you're about to marry? 'Alright, I love her?'" he asked.

"I can say a lot about her."

"Well, let's hear it."

"Hell, I breathe her in when I wake up in the morning. Her essence fills the air wherever I am, whether she is near or far. Being with her has made me come alive. She's on my mind all the time, morning, noon, and night. My body rages for her today the same way it did when we first met. I could say more, but that's the gist of how I feel."

"And you're marrying her because she does all these things to and for you?"

"That and the fact that I couldn't imagine going back to life without her. In truth Dad, I couldn't live without her even if I tried."

"That's very good, Son. Now let me ask you one more question. The way you feel about

Destiny, do you think forty years will change that?"

"I'm confident no amount of time will change the way I feel about her, even a week without her drives me up the wall," I said remembering the time after the attack, when I couldn't see her. To imagine forty years without her was torture to my soul. I looked my Dad square in the eyes and asked, "Are you saying you feel the same way about Ms. Clara?"

"You're damned right that's what I'm saying." Dad ran his fingers through his hair. "Does it make me feel good to know I'm a married man whose heart has been owned by another woman for all these years? No. But it's the way I feel and I can't deny the way I feel."

"This is deep, Dad. You admitting this is going to change everything for our family."

"I know and I'm sorry, but what you feel for Destiny multiplied by forty is how long and hard I've loved Clara Baker."

I couldn't believe Dad was talking about the same woman who'd been evil enough to conspire with Destiny's ex-husband, Montie, to keep me away from Destiny when she was in the hospital. The woman who'd been a thorn in my side during a tough time. Then it hit me. Clara didn't want Destiny with me because of her relationship with my father. She had known who I was before I met her at the hospital.

"Back in the seventies, she was my heart," Dad said, interrupting my thoughts. "I thought those feelings had wasted away, until I laid eyes on her again. Clara was a feisty little thing, but she was as sweet as they came when she was with me. I think I feel even stronger for her now."

"But how can you be sure? Forty years is a lot of time. People change over the years. I think you need to take some time to get to know her and her quirks, before you jump ship."

Start here "Son, had I had enough heart years ago, I'm one hundred percent sure you and Destiny would be siblings. I would have been with Clara, exactly the woman she is today. I'm just glad you had the courage to follow your heart, which strangely enough led you to where I left mine."

"Mom's heart is breaking right now," I said, knowing some of the heartache she brought upon herself.

"I assure you that *if* your mother's heart is breaking, it's not for the reasons you think."

"You have to do something to make this right, Dad. She may be hard around the edges, but she loves you. She's still my mother and, no matter what she does, I don't want to see her hurt," I said realizing my parents may be at the end of their marital rope.

Dad pressed the button on the lamp twice to bring extra light into the room. There was a haggard look on his face. "I know you love her. I love her too. But we can't keep excusing the hurtful things she does. Your mother is a hurt person who hurts others, and I think that hurt stems from feeling trapped in a loveless marriage for almost forty years. She has hopes and dreams that she didn't follow, too. I think they've caught up with her and made her bitter."

"Well, I never heard Mom talk about anything but proper etiquette, dinner parties and galas. I imagined her dream was to be Queen Elizabeth or something," I said on a slight laugh, as I remembered Mom's elegant tendencies. "What dreams did she have other than being elegant?"

"Much like my parents, Tammy's parents had two things they wanted most. They wanted her to marry someone of the opposite sex and of the white race. So, when Papa Turner hired her father as an engineer for Turner Enterprises back in 1965, I think he started planning my future family then. It didn't help that Tammy's father went on to create ground-breaking construction tools and methods that made Turner Enterprises lots of money. Since my mother and Tammy's mother were good friends and our fathers were in the same business, it was just natural to pair us together."

"Well, did you want to date Mom?" I asked.

"She was fun to date, but I wanted a full life experience. I couldn't see myself being tied down to a handpicked wife, at the time. I wanted to see what the world had to offer. So, I talked my parents into letting me go to college at Wellmington, where I could find my own identity."

"Wellmington, the community college? I thought you went to Yale."

"I did, but your old man went to Wellmington first. It was back in the days when Wellmington was a university. It didn't become a community college until it reopened in 1996."

"I can't believe Papa Turner was fine with you going to Wellmington." I said in disbelief. I remembered my grandfather being adamant about me going to Yale, when I graduated high school. And just the thought of the rundown Wellmington buildings probably made Papa Turner cringe.

"Yeah, Papa didn't think the college was up to the par for his son. Nonetheless, it was where I wanted to go and I was adamant, so eventually he agreed. I had to promise I would keep a 4.0 GPA and take my graduate classes at a school of his choosing though."

"I assume you met Clara at Wellmington?"

"And fell so crazy in love with her," Dad said as he thought back to the day he fell for Ms.

Clara. I watched my father stare longingly at the ceiling, as if he were remembering every moment exactly as it was. “We were inseparable,” he finally added.

“I see,” I said before pausing. “But what were Mom’s hopes and dreams? What is it that she left unfulfilled?” I asked, in attempt to bring him back to the reality that he had a wounded wife sleeping under this same roof.

“Your Mom wanted to dance.”

“Dance?”

“She wanted to go to Broadway and dance on the grandest stages alongside the greatest dancers.”

“Did she ever make it to Broadway, at least for an audition?”

“No, her father thought her dancing around the country was the silliest thing he’d ever heard. He told her story after story about women who left the south headed north or out west looking for fame. He discouraged her from pursuing her dancing dream, told her to find a good man who could afford to take care of her, and to put her energy toward being the best housewife, and that’s what she did.”

It was disheartening to hear the pain in my father’s voice as he spoke about Mom’s unfulfilled dreams. “So, your heart was with another woman and Mom’s heart was on

Broadway?" I asked, with the full understanding that my golden-aged parents had yet to live the lives they truly desired.

"Yes."

Upon hearing his admission, I was glad I was a man who went after what he wanted and grabbed it by the horns. I couldn't imagine suppressing the overwhelming feeling that came over me when I first saw Destiny walking out of Tazi's in Atlanta. I very well could have walked on by and minded my own business. I could've ignored the insatiable draw that pulled me to her, but I went after what I wanted and I didn't give a damn who knew it. If I'd walked on by, I wouldn't have experienced some of my best moments of my life.

"How did you make it so many years with neither of you fulfilling your dreams? I don't get it."

"Your mother and I, we had some happy years. We adjusted our dreams and created a new norm, which included making a fortune for our family business and, of course, creating you," Dad said with a smile. "You have always been a bright spot in my life. I've always loved you, Son."

"I love you too, Dad. But I don't want to see Mom hurt. She has given her life to this marriage. It's all she knows."

"I've considered that, just as I've considered many other things. Just because we spent our lives making unfulfilled investments doesn't obligate us to continue making deposits in that same account for the rest of our lives. It's never too late to truly live, and that's what seeing Clara made me realize."

"I wish I had a comeback for that, but that is a good point," I said on a sigh. "I support you in whatever you decide."

"Thanks, Son, because how I feel is final. Things may seem weird at first, it may hurt even, but it's for the best," Dad said standing up. "Now, come on, let's go get some rest. Tomorrow is the first day of the rest of our lives."

Weariness shadowed his face as we walked out of his study, but there was also a glow of relief starting to shine through. I felt a little better after talking to him. I still didn't want to see my parents split over Dad being in love with my soon to be mother-in-law.

Chapter 1

Jacob

After the Love is Gone

When I walked into the setting room the next morning after that horrible dinner debacle, the air of bitterness was all around Mom. One by one, she snapped at the maid, hollered at the cook, and was about to tell the gardener to redo the entire flower garden before I stepped in. Mom was taking no prisoners as she popped off one order after the next.

"Mickey, I don't know what you were thinking when you planted my rose bushes so close to the road. I want you to go out there and take every last one of them up and make sure you redo the grass surrounding them too. And do not make my lawn look like a mess! Do you hear me?" Mom said.

"But Ma'am, you're the one who told me..." Mickey started to say in his defense.

"Do you hear me?" Mom screamed at the top of her lungs, shutting him up before turning her fury to Greta. "And Greta, you know I have allergies!"

"Greta, Mickey, it's been a rough morning for Mom. You two can go back to your regular duties and we'll let you know if we need any other special duties done today," I said nodding in their direction.

"Yes, Sir," Greta and Mickey said in unison as they eased out of the room.

"Thanks for all you do," I said with a forced smile, before turning my attention to Mom.

"You have no right to interrupt me! I am the lady of this house and I know how I want things done," Mom ranted.

"Yeah, but there is no reason for you to talk to Mickey like that and Greta has been nothing but kind to you all these years. She doesn't deserve your wrath either."

"If they want to keep their stinky little jobs, they will do what I say and when the hell I say it, Jacob." Mom stormed toward the doorway and screamed Greta's name. "Greta, get back in here now!"

Greta hadn't made it completely out of sight, so she stopped in her tracks and looked back at me. I waved her on and she sped off toward the kitchen and dashed around the corner.

"Greta! I know you heard me. If you don't get back in here this instance."

"Stop it, Mom. You are taking your anger out on the wrong people."

"No, I'm not. You should see the dust I found on the baseboard behind the sofa, and she knows I have bad allergies! Get back in here, Greta," she said before turning her nose up in the air with distaste.

"And you moved the sofa to look for dust, because..."

"I am not upset with your Father, if that's what you're thinking. He just has some misguided thoughts and feelings right now, but don't be mistaken. I have your Father wrapped around my finger," she said pointing out her diamond covered ring finger. "Now like I was saying, what I'm upset about is that we pay our help so much and they can't do something as simple as laying a flower bed or dusting."

"Sure," I said as I sat down on the sofa and picked up a magazine. I haphazardly browsed the magazine while she continued to rant.

"Jacob, I want you to know that I'm unbothered by anything *those people* came in here to do last night."

"That's the problem," I said placing the magazine back on the table. "You should be bothered. The thoughts and feelings you're unbothered by are serious to me and Dad. If there is any chance for you to salvage the relationships with your son and husband, you're going to have to understand those facts."

"Jacob, you do not know what you're talking about," Mom yelled with venom spewing from her eyes.

"Mom, calm down and talk to me. Right now, I'm actually on your side when it comes to saving your marriage. The last thing I want to see is my parents divorced."

"Fine. You want to know how I really feel about last night?"

"Amongst other things, I do want to know how you feel about last night."

"I feel like it's your fault for bringing *those people* into our home and upsetting our family. Of all the black people in this highly populated world, how could you go out and handpick Clara's daughter?"

"*Those people* did not upset our family. If anything, Clara coming back into the picture only shined a light on what was already wrong. For instance, before you even knew Ms. Clara was coming to dinner, you had already planned to disrespect my fiancé by inviting Justine." Mom huffed and turned her back on me. "But, if it makes you feel any better, I didn't know about Dad and Clara's history. I found out the same time you did," I said, knowing that I didn't owe her any type of explanation after the way she treated me and Destiny.

"Well, that makes me feel a whole heap better," she said sarcastically, before turning back to face me.

"Mom, no matter what has transpired here, I'm marrying Destiny and she will be a part of this family. In order for it to work, you have to show some damn respect. Your attitude towards her is getting old."

"You don't even understand what you've done," she said, throwing her hands in the air and hitting them hard against her legs when they came down. "Your father slept in the guestroom last night, because he's pining over a forty-year-old love affair. You brought the woman it took me years to extract from his heart into our home. You don't know how he used to call out for her in his sleep. Do you know what it took for him to get her out of his system? Do you know how many times I've caught him looking at her old pictures, Jacob? To this day, he has an album labeled Wellmington memories."

"Mom, listen."

"And now, at sixty five years old, I had to watch him stand in front of her acting like he never knew my name. Like he's twenty again. And you seem to think we'll just get through this?"

I listened to my mother and couldn't help but feel torn. On the one hand, after years of idle stability, my parent's marriage was in a rocky place. On the other hand, she had some nerve to look to me for sympathy after her blatant disregard for my relationship.

At that moment, I hated that my mother didn't like Destiny. That my father had a past with Ms. Clara. That Ms. Clara slapped my father in front of everyone. That Justine was at dinner. That Justine's actions caused a rift in my relationship with Destiny, which left the back door open for Montie to slide in. But most of all, I didn't like that Mom was hurting. At the end of the day, she was the first woman who ever had my heart.

Watching Mom's tears fall counterbalanced my reluctant acceptance of Dad's feelings for Clara, the woman he claimed was his one true love. Thinking back, I watched Dad spend countless amounts of emotional energy trying to please Mom in one way or another. He would wine and dine her, and buy her special gifts. He catered to her every want and need, as far as my youthful eyes could see. However, she would only reward him with an artful smile, a kiss, or more requests for things she wanted.

Sometimes, I would see him look at her as she rambled on about new items she purchased or planned to purchase and I would see an empty expression behind his eyes, a longing. Mom didn't even notice the longing. She just navigated through, making her best effort at becoming the perfect, high-class housewife.

What I knew for sure, as I listened to Mom ramble on about Ms. Clara being at dinner, was that my father longed for the moment he shared with Ms. Clara. He appreciated holding her in his arms as much as his next breath. As a man who went from a relationship of convenience with Justine into a whirlwind romance with Destiny, I understood my father's position.

Nevertheless, Mom had one thing over Ms. Clara, and that was forty years of matrimony. I just hoped she managed to pull herself together fast enough to express genuine love, before all was lost.

"Mom, I need you to listen to me and listen to me very closely. Do you hear me? Very closely," I said as I patted a place on the sofa for her to sit next to me.

She sighed as she relented. When she sat down next to me, I leaned toward her and engaged her as intimately and caring as a son could. She looked at me willfully, and I hoped the layers of her nasty, high-society attitude would peel back as I spoke. I needed to get to the core of the woman who had meager beginnings in a small town in Alabama before moving to Miami, when her father got a job promotion.

"I'm listening," she said, nudging me to continue.

"For me, I demand that you set aside any and all ill-feelings you have for Destiny. That will be necessary for us to have any semblance of a relationship in the years to come. For Dad, you need to figure out a way to get inside his heart again. Make him remember why he chose to marry you. Because what I saw last night was not a man who was intruded upon by unwanted guests."

I stopped right there. I dared to tell Mom I saw love, compassion and hope in my father's eyes. A look that let me know for a fact he never stopped loving Ms. Clara one minute. I was sure Mom saw it too. I couldn't remember a time when he looked at her that way.

Mom considered what I was saying and dropped her hands to her side. "Jacob, there are a lot of things you don't understand about me and your father. We may not have had a fiery romance, but we've grown old together. We will be just fine."

"I wouldn't be so sure about us, Tammy," Dad said as he walked into the room.

"Johnny?" Mom said jumping to her feet.

"You can sit back down, Tammy. You've done enough jumping around and having your say," Dad said.

"I will do no such thing," Mom said in defiance.

"Sit down, Tammy!" Dad's voice boomed through the room.

Mom's back was as straight as a board and her face was as red as a beet as she glared at my father. However, under his harsh tone Mom's body inched down onto the sofa to sit as she was told. "I'm sitting down, now what is this foolishness you're saying? What do you mean you wouldn't be so sure of us?"

"Son, would you excuse us? We need to talk for a minute."

"Sure," I said standing to leave. "Mom and I were just finishing up our conversation about last night. We'll talk more about it later," I said to Mom who twirled her head in the opposite direction.

"I'm going to get to the bottom of everything that happened yesterday. You can believe that," Dad said, giving me a nod.

"Alright, well, I'll see you later," I said including both of my parents in my gaze.

Dad nodded as I walked through the door, while Mom ignored me. From the way she was acting, I knew she would never change. Left to her own devices, she would essentially put the last nail in her own coffin. Therefore, I told myself I would be at peace with whatever they decided to do.

Chapter 2

John Turner

I Wish You Well

"Tammy, there is no nice or neat way to say what I have to say," I said walking into the room. I could feel knots forming in my stomach as I prepared to talk to my wife of forty years.

"Well, just say it already, John."

"This marriage is over."

"What? Our marriage is not over! You can't mean a word you're saying," Tammy said scooting to the edge of her seat.

"Tammy, I don't want this situation to get any uglier than it has to. It's not like every other memory I have of you hasn't already been bad enough. Let's just cut our losses and call it quits, so we can spend our golden years happy. We don't have to pretend to be happy any longer."

"But... I'm not pretending. I am happy, John. I am happy to be Mrs. Turner, always have been." A slight smile crept upon Tammy's pouty lips as she said my last name.

Any other time, I probably would have let her admission slide right on past me. I would have extracted what I wanted to hear from her statement. But this time, I heard what she was really saying. Being a part of the Turner legacy made her happy. Being my wife was simply collateral to owning the name.

"I've been content with you being happy for so many years, which is why I've always given you what you wanted. I let you have free reign to live whatever kind of life you wanted to live, Tammy," I said as I scanned the various expensive items in our guest living room.

A ten thousand dollar grandfather clock, a five hundred thousand dollar sofa that was originally owned by General George Washington and countless other heirlooms that served for empty conversation at cocktail parties. I remembered the thrill Tammy had as she purchased each item. It was a joy she reserved for guests at her many gatherings hosted in our home, ritzy weddings we attended, or when she was ordering more things for this house. Things that didn't mean a thing to me. Hell, the delivery drivers had received more longing and loving looks than I had over the years, as they ushered in her many prized possessions.

"This is the end of the road for me. I don't have anything left to give to you," I continued.

"I don't need anything else, John. I have everything I could ever want," she said as she stood and walked over to me. Her eyes pleaded to the softer side of me.

No matter what bad feelings I had about our marriage, Tammy was still the woman I'd spent the last forty years with. It was hard to say, "I don't have what I want though. To be honest, as long as we've been married I've never had what I wanted."

A look of hurt flashed across Tammy's face before she replaced it with her signature half smile. She was fishing for control as she tilted her head slightly to say, "What more could you possibly want, John? We have more than anyone could ask for. We have a wonderful son, a beautiful life and a marvelous home."

"Well, let's talk about it. You've crossed our son in more unconscionable ways over the past months than I care to mention. Our life was built on lies, so our foundation has forever been weak. The only thing I can say that you have cherished is our home."

"That's not true. I have cherished you, too."

"You don't even know me, Tammy."

She waved me off and rolled her eyes. This conversation was peeving her and I was sure she thought this too would blow over and she'd be back to vintage shopping, tea parties, and wreaking havoc in no time.

"I do know you, John. I know you well enough to know you'll be back to your senses soon," she said.

"Tammy, look, I'm not going to do this with you. I've never been a man of many words, so I don't intend to argue with you. However, I encourage you to take my words at face value. When I tell you it's over, please understand our marriage is over."

"It's not..." Tammy said faintly before her words trailed off.

"We've come to the end of the road."

Tammy stepped closer to me. "Please, John."

"The way you treated our son's fiancé was the last straw."

Her face wrinkled into a deep frown. "So this is about that untrained heifer that came into our home and acted like she just got out of the zoo? Hmph, I guess she had no choice. Her mother swings from the same branch. Both of them are donkey asses in my opinion." I glared at Tammy and she backed down. "John, I'm sorry. Maybe I shouldn't have said that. I just know we can get past everything that happened at dinner. All we have to do is keep those people out of our house."

"Our house," I said as I imagined hearing Clara's laughter bounce from the walls of the room we were standing in. "Tammy, you will never be able to undo enough of the damage you've caused in order to measure up to the woman you call an animal."

"I knew it! I knew this was all about that damn Clara."

"Part of it is," I admitted.

"Oh, Johnny, you think you still love her?" Tammy laughed. "You're an old man still auditioning for a part in the Romeo play. This is all really cute."

"Only a woman who has never loved her husband would make jokes and think this matter is cute."

"It's cute because you walked away from her forty years ago and now all of a sudden you're in love."

"Well, let's see how cute it is when I divorce you and move her into this house."

"Try it and I will own Turner Enterprises outright," Tammy said.

"You can talk about our marriage and try whatever you want, but when it comes to my business you already know you are locked out of any type of payday, so I don't know why you're exciting yourself with the idea of owning Turner

Enterprises," I said coolly. On any given day, Tammy and I had ninety nine problems, but her taking my business would never be one.

"You think you have everything working in your favor, huh? We'll see about that, Johnny."

"I'm not going to entertain any ideas you may have about Turner Enterprises. And what I feel for Clara is well above your ability to understand. I never stopped loving her, not for one minute."

"Johnny, don't you say these things to me! You can't love her. You married me, remember? Must I pull out the photo albums and remind you who you are, who you've been for the past four decades?"

"That won't be necessary. I know who I am… a man who made choices based upon what his family and society had to say. I married you because my father insisted you were the one for me."

"Rubbish, we dated and you asked me to marry you because you wanted to marry me. No one twisted your arm, so don't rewrite our history."

"Tammy, I was trying to get Clara out of my heart back then. You helped ease the pain, but your friendship never healed my wounds. I spent all these years with a Band-Aid over a wound that needed surgery. Seeing Clara last night and holding her in my arms was like finding a surgeon who offered a procedure that could heal me, at last. I have to get her back, so I can finally heal."

The weight of my words caused Tammy to back away from me and shrink down into her chair once again. Her gaze was distant as she recounted our life together.

"Forty years, I have given forty years to you. I could have danced amongst the greats. I could have opened my own studio. I could have done a lot of great things with my life, but I spent my best years with you."

"All you have to do is listen to your words. What's inside will come up. You just said you could've been doing something great, but instead you were with me."

"I didn't mean it like that," she said moving forward in her seat. I held up a hand to stop her from rising.

"I don't blame you for your regrets. You should've been doing what you loved many years ago," I said as I looked into her aged eyes that had grown so weary. "We both made sacrifices and put aside what we really wanted to make our parents happy. We gave all we were capable of giving to each other. But for how much time must we sacrifice fire-burning, passionate love?"

"Well, what more do you expect from me, John? I tried my best to love you."

"You don't have to try when it's love, Tammy," I said, feeling pained over her statement, and the time we both lost.

"It's not like we had the ideal love story. You know how bad I wanted to move to New York, but my father wanted me to stay and marry you. I did what I thought was best. And I thought we had grown to love each other."

"The bar was set so low for love that we both failed to realize we were not giving or receiving genuine love. What we have done is learned to tolerate each other. Our fathers gelled us together and we could have crafted anything we wanted from that gel. But with your desire to have money, power and status, and with my heart filled with another woman, there was no room for our love to develop."

"I didn't desire money, power, and status."

"You're using your money, power, and status to humiliate Destiny. That's why it's so easy for you to dismiss her and invite the woman who is wreaking havoc on his life into our home. Never mind that Justine extorted money from my company by seducing the best damn VP of Finance the company has ever had. She did it all to spite our son and your allegiance to her has brought spite to us all. The concept of genuine love doesn't register well with you."

Tammy began wringing her hands together. Her voice shook as she said, "I may have gotten that one wrong, Johnny, but Justine just needs some mental help and she's going to get through this. You'll see."

"Is that why you put the judge in your pocket who gave her special treatment in that Atlanta courthouse? You didn't think I knew that, did you?" I asked. "I know every damn thing that happens in this family, even about your hidden bank accounts."

Tammy's eyes doubled in surprise, when I mentioned her accounts. "Those are just savings accounts, just so I can easily access the money in case something happened to you."

"Millions of dollars that you're saving! Money you've siphoned from our joint accounts and stowed away as if it's your own personal money, Tammy?"

"I can have it back in our account tomorrow, if it's that serious, John" Tammy said.

"Keep it, along with the settlement my lawyer is preparing for you," I said, walking over to pour a glass of scotch. I didn't usually drink so early in the day, but my nerves were in a bundle.

"A lawyer! You can't be fucking serious about this," Tammy yelled as she stormed toward me. "Now, Johnny, you are going too far for these damn niggers."

I turned just as she was about to raise her hand to touch me and pushed her away. Her hands fell to her sides as I glared at her. "You are a sad excuse for a human being," I said just as she started to say something else. "Earlier you asked me what more could I possibly want. I'll tell you what I want. I want someone who looks at me after forty years and slaps the taste out of my mouth with so much passion that I remember a time when I loved so deeply that it hurt. I want a woman who stops time when I'm with her, and that's what Clara does for me. So call her whatever you want, they are just words, but from this day forward never call yourself my wife, again."

"Oh, hogwash! This is all a bunch of puppy love foolishness, Johnny. We are well into our sixties. We're too old for bullshit!"

"If that's foolishness and bullshit, say one thing about us that tops what I just said about Clara?" I waited a few seconds for an answer. "Okay, I'll make this easy for you. When was the last time you told me you loved me?"

Tammy looked away from me as if the thought of saying I love you and looking at me couldn't exist in the same space. "I said it to you a thousand times since we've been married."

"But when was the last time, Tammy?"

"Johnny, I've said it to you."

"Here, I'll make this even easier for you. When was the last time you kissed me? Not a peck on each cheek like you would give any notable person, but a soul-stirring, warm-blooded kiss. When was the last time we shared something like that, huh?"

"Johnny, stop it. You know I don't have a problem kissing you."

I stepped closer to her and took her hand into mine. I pulled her toward me and looked into her eyes, searching the windows of her soul looking for the woman I asked to marry me. The woman who my parents thought was my perfect helpmate. The woman who I'd talked to hours on end when I was purging lingering thoughts of Clara Baker from my mind and heart.

In our own time, Tammy and I shared ideas, dreams and laughter. We had a connection once. When I thought I found that connection by looking in her eyes, I pulled her toward me for a kiss. Her head turned slightly and that kiss landed on her cheek.

"You see, this really isn't a hard choice to make, Tammy. Our bed, as well as our hearts, has been cold for a long time. Like I said, my lawyer will get your paperwork to you as soon as possible." Tammy stood there looking at me with a blank expression, so I continued. "You can take anything you bought over the years with you and you will get a handsome settlement. And, I wish you well," I said as I turned to walk out the room.

"John, I am not divorcing you. Our fortieth anniversary gala is this year and I've already told my friends about it."

"Call them back," I tossed over my shoulder as I went into my study and locked the door.

Chapter 3

John

Family Business

I had no regrets as I rattled off the details of my divorce to my lawyer. "Yeah, a fifty million dollar lump sum and twenty thousand a month for the rest of her life," I told him.

"Are you sure this is what you want to do?" he asked.

"Just get it done," I said running my free hand across my beard.

"Okay Mr. Turner, I'll get this drawn up for you immediately. Call me if you want to change anything."

"Will do," I said as I hung up the phone. I felt as if a weight had been lifted off me with this move. It was a necessary for me to live out the remainder of my days without being chained to the farce I allowed to take place so many years ago. My mind traveled to the day that changed the *course of my life. The day that led up to this very moment.*

It was a warm spring morning in April of 1972, when I walked into my father's office at the original Turner Enterprise building for work. I worked Saturdays learning the family business and spending time with my father. This Saturday, I was a few minutes late, since I stopped by Clara's house to take her some breakfast.

Within seconds of walking through the door, my father started in on me. He gave me a once over and said, "Son, your mother tells me you've been hanging out with a young lady by the name of Clara Baker. Is that correct?"

I knew where the conversation was going. I'd just told my mother about Clara the night before. What I wanted her to do was soften my father for me. He always took things better when they came from her first. And my mother understood and appreciated my first love, at least that's what I thought.

"That's right, Pops. I met her at Wellmington," I answered without going into any details.

"Oh, really? Where does she live?" he asked, with a raised brow. Soon, Pops' hand stopped moving across his desk calculator and I had his undivided attention.

"Over on Westside Road near the Rapids Pond," I said, walking further into the office and sitting down on the sofa. I leaned forward raptly,

waiting to see where he would carry the conversation.

Over the years, Pops had drilled into me that people needed to stick with their own kind. Therefore, I didn't know how he would take it if he knew I had every intention to make the very dark and lovely, Clara Baker, my wife.

"Well, I invited Tammy Jentry to our house for dinner tonight. I think it's time that you start spending time with a more suitable mate, and Tammy is a good, fine choice."

"I already have plans for tonight," I told my father.

"Well, this is my first time hearing of you having plans. I guess you can just reschedule whatever you were going to do. Our dinner plans are already set."

I could feel the muscles in my neck tense up. Clara wanted to go see the new Foxy Brown movie at the drive-in, and I'd be damned if I was going to miss an opportunity to have her curled up in my arms feeding me popcorn and soda to be at a stuck up dinner with my parents and the Jentry family.

My father continuously dropped hints about me dating his colleague's daughter, Tammy. She was a beautiful brunette with Marilyn Monroe features that had, at one time, caught my attention. However, she was such a stick in the mud that even her looks didn't hold my attention for long. It was Clara's natural beauty, big smile, and even bigger personality that snatched me up and held me captive.

The first day I met Clara she was in the registration line with her parents at Wellmington College. I was walking out of one of the administrative offices with my parents.

"Are you sure you want to register for this school, John?" my father had asked as we walked to the end of the registration line.

"Yes, I'm sure," I said as Clara and I made eye contact. She was a standout girl wearing a warm colored plaid skirt suit and high platform shoes. Her pretty, brown eyes peeked from underneath her cloche hat. As I walked by, I smiled and she smiled back.

My father and I completed registration and I finally got my dorm assignment. I set out to find out more about the girl with the pretty, brown eyes. I asked a few people in the girls' dormitory if they'd seen a girl who matched her description, but no one knew who I was talking about.

Just when I thought I'd never see her again, I walked into my English class a week later and she was sitting in the front row. Her light brown legs were crossed at the ankle. She was wearing a pink ruffled blouse and a black pencil skirt. She had on a pair of thick rimmed glasses and her hair was pulled back in a curly puff to the side with a pink ribbon holding it in place.

I took my seat and began to listen to our teacher present her first lecture. All the while, I couldn't keep my eyes off Clara. Even from behind, she looked so good. She sat up proper in her seat. She studiously took notes. She engaged the professor by raising her pencil to ask questions. I was intrigued with her every move.

After class was over, I asked if she would mind studying together. At first, she refused, but I was adamant that we could help each other in the class. We set a date for our first study session and I set out to win her heart. Despite her many objections and reasons we should both stay in our perspective worlds, I proved to her time and time again that we were meant to be together.

"John-John, please don't ever hurt me," she pleaded the night I savored every moment of her sweet virginity.

"I would never hurt you, Clara. I only want to love you forever," I replied as I kissed her sweet lips and eased into her warmth for the most fulfilling ten minutes of my life.

Therefore, as I sat on the sofa that Saturday morning in my father's office, I thought about my words to Clara. The promise I made before consummating our love meant more than what my father was asking me to do. I had no intention to ever hurt Clara, especially if it was to spend time with Tammy Jentry and her parents over dinner.

"I'm not going to be home until after dinner tonight, Dad," I said, as my father and I were headed out after a productive Saturday morning's work.

He looked at me with disappointment. "You need to consider the choices you're making these days very closely, Son," he said as we parted ways.

"I am," I said wondering if he would ever understand the way I felt.

I took Clara to see Foxy Brown that night and we made love in the back seat of my old Chevy as the movie played out on the big screen. I was so happy when I walked her to her parents' door and gave her a kiss goodnight. But when I got back home, Pops kept me up much of the night talking about the controversy my relationship with Clara could cause. He said being with her was a death sentence over my life, career, and everything I held dear. He even said we could lose our family business, or even worse I could end up dead because of my relationship with Clara.

My father knew how much I loved our family business, how much I believed in our family's legacy. He knew because he instilled it in me since I was old enough to walk. He knew if anything would get to me, the loss of my grandfather's business might snap me back to the reality of the world we lived in. One of tight-lipped segregation in an officially desegregated society. One of evil that lurked in the nooks and crevices of America.

I held steadfast to my love for Clara, even when my father threatened not to pay my tuition for the following semester and to move me to another school in another state. And when my first semester at Wellmington ended, so did my financial support for that small, fine institution. My father had his own plan. He had pulled some strings and enrolled me at Yale University.

"You might as well go and tell that girlfriend of yours it's over. It will be years before you get to see her again, if I have anything to do with it," he told me as he held the acceptance papers for Yale in his hands about a month later. "Besides, once you get to Yale and start hanging around those kids, you will have forgotten everything about Wellmington."

I put two and two together really fast. My father didn't want me to be with Clara, so he was moving me clear across the country to Yale. I didn't want to leave Clara, but I had no choice if I wanted to finish college and not bring shame to my family for being a bum.

She was heartbroken when I told her I was moving to another state to finish college. She knew my father disapproved of her and blamed me for giving up so easily. "You say you want to be with me and you don't want to leave. If you really want to be with me, you would fight for us," she'd said.

"I can't make my father pay for Wellmington. If I could afford to pay for my own tuition, I would stay," I tried to reason with her. I didn't want to leave. I wanted to fight for us. But I did what most young men did in the seventies. I did what my father asked of me. I assimilated into the world that was created many years before I was born.

Seeing how devastated she was and not knowing when we'd get to see each other again, I reluctantly broke things off. I wanted her to find someone to make her happy, someone that wasn't thousands of miles away, and someone that wasn't off limits to her in society's eyes.

When I came back home for spring break, Clara wouldn't accept my calls and told her mother not to allow me near their house. Eventually, I stopped bothering her. I felt there was nothing I could say or do to ease her pain but leave her alone. I told her I would never leave her and never hurt her, but I did.

Out of need for companionship, I took Tammy out on a date. One date led to two and before I knew anything, I was standing at the altar waiting for my bride to enter the chapel. When I pulled the veil from over Tammy's head to kiss her, I closed my eyes and imagined it had been Clara's pretty, brown eyes staring back at me. That was the day I signed away forty years of my life to a loveless marriage. It was the day I sealed my fate.

I tried like hell to forget Clara. I tried even harder to remember Tammy was the one I was supposed to love and cherish each day of my life. It was a goal I never reached. A goal I never wanted to reach.

Chapter 4

Destiny

Leave Well Enough Alone

While I could've lived my entire life and not seen Jacob's mother again, my own mother had a few surprises up her sleeve, as well. She had some real explaining to do, once we touched down in Atlanta. I had the limo drive us to her house, where I was staying the night so she could answer the many questions running through my mind. The whole fiasco at Jacob's parents' house opened up chapters I had never read about my own mother.

I was sitting at her kitchen table with my foot in the chair. My chin rested on my knee, with my arms wrapped around my leg, as I was in deep thought.

"Don't sit over there looking at me like that Destiny," Mama said after fixing herself a cup of hot tea.

"Mama, you knew all along that Jacob's father was the original heir of Turner Enterprises. So you knew when we left your house with your flowers that you would be going to the Turner's home and that you would see Mr. Turner there."

"Of course, I knew," Mama said as she placed her tea on the table and sat across from me.

"So you planned for this mess to happen?"

"It's been forty years since I saw that man. I didn't expect anything to happen, except dinner."

"Why didn't you just come out and tell me you'd been in a relationship with Jacob's father? You spent all this time talking down about Jacob and, come to find out, it stems from whatever his father did to you."

"When the kids first started talking about you dating a white man from Miami named Jacob and all the gifts he was buying them and trips he was taking them on, the first person I thought about was John. I knew he had a son named Jacob. I was hoping it was some great big ole' coincidence, so I started researching Jacob then."

"You did research on Jacob?"

"Girl, I have researched every boy to man you've ever dated."

"That's a mess, Mom. I didn't know you snooped in my business like that."

Mom waved a hand at me. "When I realized he was John's son, I almost flat lined. I couldn't believe you were actually dating his son. It was more than I could handle, but I honestly didn't plan to act up at their house. I'm sorry, Destiny."

"I just can't believe you knew Jacob was John's son the entire time and you never said anything."

"What was I going to say? You're in love with the son of the man that broke my heart?"

"Well, yeah."

"I think I about lost my good sense when I found out. I didn't want you to go through the same thing I went through. Until tonight, I thought Jacob was just like his father, a man who would fold under the pressure of other people's opinion. He proved me wrong."

"Jacob is a good person. He made a bad choice once, but he has apologized and I forgave him," I said, feeling the need to set the record straight about Jacob's decision to rush to be by Justine's side the night she attacked me.

"I know that now. At the very least, he will defend your honor," Mama said and I figured she was making reference to the way her relationship ended with Mr. Turner.

"Is that how Mr. Turner hurt you? He didn't stand his ground for you?"

"It was definitely that, among other things. Things I don't want to resurface now, after it took me so long to heal."

"Mama, you haven't healed. If it were ever possible to carry around a grudge for over forty years, you have mastered that ability. What happened between you two is just as vivid today as it was back in the seventies."

"It may still sting, but I ain't hurting. I've been just fine without John. I'm not about to start acting like I need him now."

"Yet, you went to his house to have dinner with no forewarning, knowing his wife would be there."

"I did want to see him, but I didn't mean for there to be a confrontation. I thought I'd see him sitting at the dinner table with his loving wife and son, as they welcomed my daughter into their family. I thought I'd get to see that he had in fact grown old with the love of his life. I hoped he wouldn't even remember me, and that I'd be but a long, lost memory. I thought I'd be able to look him in the eye and that nothing would be there."

"And what good would that have done for you, Mama? If Mr. Turner had looked right through you and said 'pass the butter', it would have hurt you even more."

"No it would not have! I would've walked out of there knowing I was just a moment of his life and the love we shared wasn't real. I would've been able to reconcile those feelings with the way I felt for so long. I would've been able to file him away as another asshole without a heart who became an old fart that obliterated like the wind."

"That's not what happened, is it?" I asked, sitting on the opposite side of the table trying to keep my composure.

"No, I had no idea Justine would be there. Seeing her got my engine fired up and when John waltzed in the room, I just let him have it for both of them."

"Even as I sit here, I still can't believe Jacob's mother invited her. I just don't get that woman."

"She did it because she knew we would turn up. I might be sixty five, but I'll still kick some ass about my only child."

"I know you will, Mama." I sighed. "I guess you're right. She wanted us to act a fool so she could point her finger at us and say we were the bad apples. Why is everything getting so complicated?"

"Life is complicated. Show me someone who has an easy life and I'll show you someone who has not lived. That woman John calls a wife didn't see a problem with Justine being at that funky, no-class dinner because she doesn't have a heart. She is the epitome of the devil's daughter."

"She thinks so low of me that she invited me to sit down with a woman who almost killed me only a month ago. She hates me that much."

"Yeah, but she had the wrong ones, if she thought we was gonna sit down with the same bitch who walked away from an assault charge because of her family's money and privilege," Mama said as she slammed her mug on the table. "Ugh! Those kind of folks ain't shit. They never take responsibility for the wrath they cause."

Finally, the fury of the evening caught up with me and I let go, as well. "It was one dinner… for one damn day. She couldn't give me the dignity to sit down for one dinner without disrespecting me!"

"Chile, that woman is going to get what's coming to her and I hope I live to see it. You mark my words, she's gonna get hers," Mama said as she touched my hand.

"I don't think I'll ever get along with her, Mama. I'm done trying."

"You can get along with anyone, so you're not the problem. It's her prejudiced ways that are the problem. She decided not to give you a chance well before she knew I was your mother."

"She brings the worst out of me."

"Avoid her like the plague, Destiny. That may be best for us both, because all I know is if she comes at you wrong again I'm going to deal with her. I'm not with that old biddy disrespecting my family. You are my child and I will protect you to the death."

"Mama, this is a very fragile situation. Please promise me that you'll keep your cool too."

"I will, I don't have any intention on seeing anyone from that family again, except Jacob."

"I don't think the feeling is mutual. I saw the way John looked at you. That man is uncontrollably in love with you and he will be coming for you soon."

"John doesn't know how to love anyone. He better stay his ass in Miami, if he knows what's best for him."

"I'm all for what you want, Mama," I said before taking a closer look at her. "If that's what you want."

"It's what I want," Mama said in a softer tone. "Destiny, if John loved me, my place setting would've been on the opposite end of his chair at his dinner table. I'd be the queen of his throne. That's not the case, so don't confuse his feeling guilty for the way he walked away from me with love."

"I can't argue that point, Mama."

"And you should never argue what's real."

"Mama, don't take what I'm about to say the wrong way," I said, imagining if the tables had been turned. "I'm kind of glad you two didn't stay together. If you had, there would be no me and Jacob."

"Honey, Jacob would've been your brother."

"I know!" I laughed and shook my head at the thought.

"Seriously, I've been hard on Jacob and mostly for my personal reasons. Now that I've seen his passion for you on more than one occasion, I want you to be with him. I welcome him as my new son-in-law."

"Thanks, Mama." I got up and went around to hug her. My heart swelled to capacity as I thought about the love she lost so that I may have love. "And who knows, the end of your and Mr. Turner's book is probably being revised. What you thought was the end, might have been to be continued."

"You were a helplessly hopeful child who grew up to be a helpless romantic. Bless yo' sweet and gullible little heart," Mama said as she grabbed my cheeks.

"Whatever, I'm going to countdown on my fingers how long it takes for Mr. Turner to reach out to you, and for you to reach back."

"And you're going to run out of fingers, toes and hairs on your head while counting. I'm putting John Turner on notice. If he comes anywhere near me, I will chop him up in tiny little pieces and send him back to Tammy in a box with a card that says 'get yo man.'"

"Mama!" I hit her hand playfully. "You don't mean that."

"Of course, I don't think I mean it literally." Mama got up from the table and started walking towards her bedroom. "I just hope he stays away."

Chapter 5

Destiny

Joy Cometh in the Morning

The next morning when I woke up in Mama's bed, a mouthwatering aroma wafted into the room. "Mmmm, Mama must be in the kitchen cooking a big breakfast. It smells delicious," I said aloud, as I grabbed my cell off the nightstand. I scanned through my new messages and returned a few texts to my clients. I had just finished updating my calendar when I called Jacob.

"Hey, babe," he answered on the first ring.

"Hey yourself, how are you this morning?" I asked.

"Good, just in the office going over some files before I head back your way. How about you, babe? Did you sleep well?" he asked.

"I slept pretty good after staying up late trying to wrap my head around yesterday."

"Babe, words can't explain how upset I am. I'm so sorry that you had to go through that drama. I had a talk with Mom about Justine being at dinner and let her know that was unacceptable," he said.

"It was disheartening to watch it all unfold, when I had such high hopes of getting to know your mother. But you shouldn't be the one apologizing, Jacob. I know where your heart is."

"You better know where my heart is Destiny. But I'm obligated to protect you from things like that. It won't happen again."

"Speaking of apologies, I had a heart-to-heart with Mama last night and I'm sorry she slapped your father."

Jacob paused as if he were considering his words before speaking.

"He asked Mom for a divorce today."

"Really? Oh no, I feel so bad, Jacob," I said truly feeling like shit.

"There's nothing for you to feel bad about."

"But I do."

"I don't want you feeling any type of way about what my parents are going through, Destiny."

"Is this all about Mama coming to dinner?"

"Based on the glow around Dad when you two left last night, I'd say it had something to do with it. He talked about Ms. Clara with so much admiration last night. And this morning, he had a talk with Mom and then later waltzed into my office at Turner Enterprises and told me he was leaving Mom as if he were announcing that he was going to get a cup of coffee."

"This can't be good news. He's acting prematurely, don't you think?" I asked.

"I've never seen him this happy."

I couldn't believe I was asking, "How does your mother feel about all of this?"

"She's is taking it hard."

"A woman losing her husband is not a small thing. You should go comfort her. She may need someone to talk to," I urged.

"I'll go by there before I head back to Atlanta. I'm going to our house to meet the interior designer first. You said you want spring colors in Montana's room, right?" he asked, sounding much livelier.

I smiled at the mention of our house; I could only imagine what he was having done to it. "That's right babe and I would like a burnt orange and blue in Junior's room."

"Consider it done," he said. I could tell he was scribbling notes down as he asked, "How is Ms. Clara doing this morning?"

"Better than yesterday. I can only tell you that much. She told me she's glad she has closure now," I said, omitting the fact that Mama knew the entire time Jacob was John's son and that her going to his parents' home was calculated and planned.

"Well, from the way Dad is acting, she might as well get ready to open back up."

"Jacob, I don't think that's a good idea. Tell him to back off. Mr. Turner showing back up this late in her life will be too much for her, especially since he already has a wife. Mama can't take being jilted again."

"I wouldn't attempt to speak for Dad. He is his own man. However, from what I understand, he plans to do right by her. Just like I plan to spend the rest of my days doing right by you."

"Aw Jacob, that's sweet. I love you."

"I love you too, future Mrs. Turner."

"I still don't think it's a good idea for our parents to..." I paused as I tried to wrap my mind around my mother dating any man, much less my soon to be father-in-law.

"To what, love each other?"

"It seems unnatural."

"Destiny, that's not for us to decide. Our parents have to make their own choices in love, just like we did. Don't begrudge them out of reuniting, if the future deems it so."

"You have a point there. Well, at least, ask your father to give my mother some more time before he approaches her. Hell, he needs to give himself some time to settle things with your mother."

"I will mention it, but, again, my father is his own man."

I sighed. "Okay, I'll talk to you later," I said, beginning to miss him already as our call was coming to an end. I was eager to get my day on a roll and catch up on my advertising work, but I could have talked to Jacob most of the morning. "But do me another favor, Jacob."

"Anything."

"Be there for your mother."

"Destiny, you are right for me in every way. I knew you were the one after our first conversation. After all Mom has done, you still are concerned about her feelings."

"She is a part of you; therefore, I will love that part of her. I am all about you... Team Jacob. I will do whatever it takes to make sure you're okay. If that means encouraging you to check up on your mother, then so be it," I said, feeling somewhat responsible for his family's breakdown. After all, I was in the center of the entire mess.

"We've been through a lot over a short period of time," Jacob said. "Believe me when I say it will be greater later, my sweetheart. I don't care about the haters."

"Are you trying to be a player on this phone early in the morning?" I asked on a laugh.

Jacob laughed, as well. "I got you to laugh, so I'm not trying. I'm succeeding."

"Well, I'm going to let you get back to your business at hand. I just wanted to hear your voice before I got up out of Mama's warm bed."

"Oh, Clara is lucky. She got to sleep with you last night. I can't wait to have my turn tonight."

"That makes two of us. See you then," I said, hanging up the phone feeling reassured.

Jacob loved his parents, so I figured, deep down, he wanted them to stay together. Actually, I preferred they stayed together, as well. The last thing I wanted was Mama being tied up with Jacob's father. It just seemed out of place for our love to be all in the family like that.

My next call was to Montie to let him know I would be picking up the kids around noon. I was glad that he was at home, because I hadn't broached the subject of moving the kids to Miami with him. That was an entirely different dilemma in itself.

Once all of my business for the day was set in motion, I got out of bed and went into the bathroom to wash my face. I spruced up a bit using the personal kit I kept at Mama's house. Pulling my hair back into a messy ponytail, I stared at my image in the mirror. I meditated for a long while before I went downstairs, praying for both peace and clarity in the midst of turmoil.

When I walked into the kitchen, I almost tumbled over my feet when I saw Mr. Turner standing by the counter intently watching Mama set the table. His eyes followed the commotion and peered into mine speaking volumes that dared to leave his lips, as he stood there in limbo.

Meanwhile, Mama went about her morning duties as if he wasn't even standing there. She moved about the kitchen preparing breakfast and humming. When she did look in his direction, she looked right through him and placed a bottle of syrup in the middle of the table.

"Good morning," I said including both of them in my gaze. I walked over and gave Mama a kiss on the cheek and whispered, "What is he doing here?"

She humped her shoulders and kept moving about the kitchen. I awkwardly acknowledged Mr. Turner by saying, "Hi, uh, very good to see you here. This time, I hope it's under much better circumstances."

There was an apology in his eyes as he said, "Hi, Destiny, likewise."

"Listen, I'm sorry about the way I acted in your home. That's not the way I would have liked to meet you," I began to say. Mr. Turner raised his hand to silence me.

"There is no need for any explanations. That's why I came here this morning. I'd hoped we could wipe the slate clean and start over," Mr. Turner's attention went from me to Mama as he made that statement. I looked between the two and immediately knew they needed time alone to talk.

"It means a lot to hear you say that, thanks Mr. Turner. I really would like it if we could wipe the slate clean. Jacob and I are getting married soon and we would love it if everyone could come together, without any more drama."

"If I have anything to do with it, there won't be any more drama, young lady. I am committed to making things right, for all parties," he said, once again gazing at Mama.

Mama had her wall up and I was convinced there was nothing Mr. Turner could say to make amends for the forty years they lost – until I saw her place a third plate down on the table.

"John, you're welcome to stay for breakfast, but after that you need to be on your way," she said flippantly.

"I would love to have breakfast with you, Clara. Thank you for offering," he said gallantly moving toward the table.

"You're not having breakfast with me. You're having breakfast with your daughter-in-law," Mama said motioning toward me with her mitten. "It will be your first and last meal in this house, so eat up and enjoy. Then, get back on your big jet and fly back to Miami where you belong… with your wife."

Mr. Turner was humble as he took a seat at the table. I figured he knew as well as I did that he was fighting an uphill battle and silence was his best defense.

"Mama, you don't have to set a plate for me. I'm about to leave."

"Why are you leaving so soon?"

"I miss my babies. I told Montie I would be by there to pick up them up early," I said, even though Montie wasn't expecting me until noon. I just wanted to get out of there to give them some privacy.

"You should start your day off with a good breakfast, baby girl. Sit down and eat," Mama said pointing at one of the plates. Her eyes widened and I could tell she was coaching me to stay. "I've worked hard in this kitchen, and you really should stay and eat," she added.

Through her hard exterior, her shaking hands gave away her nervousness about being alone with Mr. Turner. I walked over to the stove and picked up a piece of bacon. I bit into it and grabbed a biscuit.

"Mmmm, I appreciate your hard work, Mama. Your food is always so delicious," I told her as I poured a glass of juice to go with my biscuit. "But I'll eat this in the car. Goodbye, Mr. Turner," I added as I kissed her on the cheek.

"Destiny, don't leave," Mama said as I blew her a kiss and walked out the door.

CHAPTER 6

Clara

Too Little Too Late

"Well, John, are you going to eat or what?" I asked as I watched him sit there playing with his food. In between moving the food around on his plate, his dazzling hazel eyes watched my every move.

"Yes, I'm going to eat. The food is delicious, by the way."

"I can't tell by the way you're playing with it."

"That's because I have something to say. I'm just thinking of the best way to put it."

"Well, you might as well say whatever it is. The clock is running out on our last meal."

I pointed to the clock on my wall. I intended to give the old geezer thirty minutes to fill his stomach and clear his mind. Then, he had to get the hell out of my house and out of my life. That's what I felt at the moment.

However, as far as his looks, he looked nothing like an old geezer. His jawline was refined, but it was still strong like it was when he was a young man. The same young man I fell in love with so many years ago. He had sprinkles of salt and pepper amongst his gray. He was still well toned with a pronounced build.

As handsome as he was, I couldn't stand to look at him much longer. I had killed off the John I remembered when he left me and I was having a harder time than I thought I would with his revival.

"Clara, after I held you last night, it was clear to me what I've been missing in my life."

If looks could kill, John's ass would've been dead on the spot. I knew like hell he didn't have the nerve to sit at my kitchen table talking about what he'd been missing. "So this epiphany came upon you last night, huh?" I asked.

"Yes, I miss you and I want you back."

"Well, bravo!" I said, as I clapped in a slow and steady motion. "Clocking in at sixty five years old, you finally figured out what you want out of life. You should really give yourself a hand," I added as I continued to clap.

"Clara, you don't have to shoot me down before I get started, especially after the way you responded to me as I held you yesterday. Your body said the same things to me that it used to, when I touched you last night. Now, today you want to act as if it was all a façade."

"You don't know jack shit about my body. And I'm not the one who's married and hitting on another person. You are the one who built a façade."

"Why are you talking like that? You never talked like this when we were together."

"Ha! That's it. I'm not the same naïve virgin you met back in seventy two. You think you know me when you don't. If you knew me, you'd know I'm a half a second from throwing these hot grits on you," I said as my hand eased to the bowl that held my grits.

Listening to John profess his love for me brought my anger to a boiling point. I had forty years' worth of pent up frustration that was ready to be unleashed upon the object of my contempt. He was sitting at my kitchen table ruining the tiny bit of peace I'd managed to weave alone.

"Clara!"

"Clara my ass, John. It's time for you to go!"

"Clara, don't make me leave right now. I want you to know just how sorry I am."

"I know you don't think I'm going to sit in here and listen to you go on about how sorry you are. On that, we both agree. Next topic," I said, easing my hand away from the bowl and picking up the spoon. I scooped some of the grits and ate them.

"I'm a good man with a good heart who made the wrong choice. When I got to the biggest crossroad in my life, I went down the wrong road."

"Is that right?" I asked nonchalantly.

"It is, and I owe you an apology. That's why I will give you as many apologies as you need, for as long as you need to hear them. But make no mistake about it, I am the furthest thing from a sorry man and you know that."

"I will not pretend to know anything about you, John. You're practically a stranger to me."

"I'll accept that, Clara," John said as he took a sip from his coffee. His hand was shaking as he placed the mug back down on the table. We sat in silence for a while before he said, "I remember seeing you in the registration line at Wellmington. I knew you were the one for me right then and there. Remember, we were both with our parents?"

"Yeah, I remember."

"I didn't have the nerve to say anything to you, until I left registration. I searched for you all over campus and then by the luck of the draw we ended up in the same English class. When we started studying together, I waited until you were ready to move me from the friend zone into the romantic zone. I waited for you then and it seems like I've waited a lifetime for this moment."

John stood up and walked toward me. I got up from my chair and moved toward the sink. "That sounds all lovey dovey and cute, except you skipped a major part of our love story. The part where you left me and married another woman."

John's expression went from pleading to sorrow. He moved closer to me as if the close proximity would alleviate his sorrow. However, I had no intention of making him feel better. "I never meant to hurt you," he said as he reached for my hand.

I glared at him in all seriousness. "If you touch me, you will walk away with one less limb than you came here with."

"Damn it, Clara! What do you want me to do? Do you want me to just go back to Miami and act like magic didn't flow between us last night? Like seeing you didn't dig up feelings I've tried to bury for so long?"

"Throw some dirt on 'em and keep 'em buried, that's what I want you to do. I want you to leave and not care, the same way you didn't care when you left me with child."

All expression left John's face, which immediately turned pale. His breathing deepened as he clutched his chest as if to manually keep his heart beating. Finally, the moment had come for him to live through the agony that never let me go. I silently reveled in every minute of his suffering. "You were pregnant, Clara?" he asked once he gained a semblance of composure.

"I was going to tell you the day you came to my house and told me you were moving away. But after I saw how easy it was for you to walk out of my life – our lives – I didn't have the nerve to tell you. There I was at that university on my parent's last dime, money they worked their entire lives to save, pregnant with a bastard child. I had no choice but to scrape and scrub, so I could get an abortion."

The agonizing thought of walking into that rusty abortion house rushed back to me and hugged me like a Grizzly. John wrapped an arm around me and touched my stomach, as if the simple act would channel him into the soul of our lost child. I was too pained to push him away. Memories of my first pregnancy always brought me to my knees.

"I should've never left you, Clara," John said, as his eyes filled with tears that dared to fall.

I stared off into space as yesteryear's feelings of abandonment crushed my heart, all over again. "Aborting our child was the hardest decision I ever made, but I was under so much pressure. When I walked into that makeshift clinic and asked for Ms. Maggie, I knew my life would forever be altered. It still haunts me today, when I wonder what our child would have looked like, what he or she would wear, or where they would work."

While thinking about my first child, John continued to hold me and I didn't resist. I accepted the temporary comfort in his arms. For once, I had someone to lean on as I shared the way I felt about my first child, whose bright smile never saw the light of day. The incomplete feeling I'd lived with since that day never stopped haunting me, and besides Ms. Maggie, I never told a soul.

Many nights I cried myself to sleep as I wondered if our precious baby would have been a boy or girl. My heart ached for the loss of my child. It also ached because the man who implanted his seed deep within me walked away as if I and his unborn child meant nothing.

I was determined to finish college, when I left that clinic devoid of the precious human life we'd conceived. I didn't even think about dating after John. I just buried my head in the books and finished at the top of my class with a degree in communications.

The thought of all I endured alone made me retract from the hold John had on me. The pain had been my comforter. I vowed to never let another man hurt me like John did and until I met Destiny's father, Weldyn, I'd never gotten close to the same hurt.

Weldyn tried his damndest to break me with his razor sharp tongue, his constant degrading words and cheating ways. He never raised his hands to hit me, but the way he looked at me and talked to me made me embrace being single. I had two strikes on love and I didn't intend to give anyone a third chance not to love me.

However, as much as he tried, Weldyn never took me as low as I was the day I walked out of that abortion clinic without my child and without the love that created it.

"If only you knew what I went through, you wouldn't have the nerve to stand here in my face asking for forgiveness," I said to John.

"Clara, I didn't know you were pregnant. If I had known my child was growing inside of you, there would've been nothing anyone would have been able to say me to keep me away, including you. I would have stayed with you and I would have raised our child as a Turner. There is no doubt in my mind about that. You should have trusted me enough to know that."

"But yet, I wasn't enough for you to stay?"

"I didn't say that."

"Yes you did. You said it with your actions when you left me."

"I didn't know you were with child."

"John, that shouldn't have mattered."

"It matters. I never would've left you to make the decision about our child alone. I take care of my responsibilities. I always have. I don't like knowing that you felt you had no one to turn to. In fact, I broke up with you because I wanted you to find someone who could be there for you while I was away."

"It's easy to say you wouldn't have left me alone now that you're not faced with the situation. What I know is your parents didn't want you falling in love with a black girl, so they yanked you back to the front of the bus and into the land of the privileged."

"My father thought sending me to Yale would put me in a better position to run our business."

"John, you are your father's only son. You would've run your family business, even if you didn't have a college education. He would've taught you the ropes. Your father sent you to Yale, so you wouldn't be chasing behind me. Period."

"Clara..." John slid an arm around my waist again and pulled me close. He buried his head in the groove of my neck, inhaling my essence as if it were his last chance. And if I had anything to do with it, it would be his last chance.

"If you're wanting me to explain away our past, I can't. At the same time, I can't put into words what you mean to me at this very moment. Give me the opportunity to show you," he said as he hugged me closer to him.

I dared to move from the warmth of his embrace as I whispered, "Just go back to your life and let me be. I was fine before you got here."

"Were you?" he asked as his lips grazed the skin of my neck with a tender kiss.

"I was... and you should leave now, John," I said, struggling to get away from him.

He held me in place. "Going back to my life as it was is not an option. Now that I have seen you again, peered into your soul, felt your body next to mine, I'll do whatever it takes to make things right."

"You can't just say things like that when there's no way you mean it, John." I pushed him away hard. "Your time is up!" I said walking to the front door.

"Will you at least sit down and let's finish the breakfast you prepared?" he asked looking at the spread on the table. "After that, I promise I'll leave."

I knew he was just trying to buy more time, but I digressed.

"Since you're suddenly hungry, hurry up and eat and then let yourself out," I said as I walked out the kitchen and up the stairs to my bedroom. It wasn't going to be easy getting rid of him, but come hell or high water the man had to go. He wasn't about to ease back up into my life, as if the last four decades had not existed.

Chapter 7

Destiny

Navigating Different Terrain

I left Mama's house headed to Montie's to get my babies. I hadn't seen them in a few days, so I was elated when I pulled up and saw Junior playing catch with his father. Montana was sitting on the porch playing with one of her American Girl dolls. It looked as if she was having one of the grandest tea parties ever as she placed a teacup in front of each doll.

"Mommy!" Junior and Montana said in unison as I walked around my parked car.

"Hey mommy's babies. Did you miss me?"

"I miss you awot," Montana said clinging onto her doll. "My frins miss you too," she said pointing to her dolls.

"Aw, honey, I'm so ready to get home so we can play games and watch movies with your friends. You want to do that?" I asked Montana.

"Yay! I bout to go home, so I gotta get all my twoys up," she said, smiling at Montie.

"Hey, Mom, you wanna see me throw the ball fifteen feet?" Junior said once he hugged me and ran back over to pick up the football.

"Sure, babe," I told him. "Let's see what you got."

Junior picked up the ball and hurled it a nice distance. Montie stood off to the side watching him put his training to work.

"Hi, Montie," I said before walking up to the porch to help Montana pick up her toys.

"I didn't realize you were coming so early, or else I would've gotten them ready. I promised Junior I would work on his arm and we were just getting started," he said sounding a little irritated.

"That's fine, Montie, I'm not in a rush. You can go ahead and practice with him and I'll sit here with Montana, if that's okay with you," I said as I sat down on the lounger and picked up one of the doll's brushes.

"I guess that's fine, as long as it won't become a problem later with your husband," he said with a smirk.

I wondered what was really going on with his attitude change. "It won't be a problem," I assured him.

Montie went back to tossing the ball with Junior and Montana caught me up on the details of her weekend. After about thirty minutes, he gave Junior his final throw and they huddled to discuss what would make him better. Junior listened closely to his father, shaking his head as he took every word in. It was a blessing that Montie was so active in our children's lives; he really was a great father. I got a little sad as I thought about how rare these moments would be once the kids and I moved to Florida.

"I'll go get their bags, Destiny," Montie said as he and Junior jogged to the porch.

I stood up and said, "Actually I need to talk to you about something. Will it be okay if I come in to talk for a second?"

Montie shot me a suspicious look. "O-kay, that'll give the kids time to finish putting their puzzle together. They were working on it earlier," he said, walking into the house.

"Yes!" Junior said as he raced off to the half-done puzzle lying on the coffee table in the living room.

"I do the flower," Montana said, her Pull-Up whooshing loudly as she followed behind Junior. I smiled as she waddled over and picked up a puzzle piece.

Once the kids were occupied, I settled in a chair in the kitchen. It was an open area, so we were able to keep an eye on the children as we talked. Montie poured himself a glass of water.

"Would you like anything to drink?" he asked, tilting a glass in my direction.

"Nah, I'm good, Montie."

"What's on your mind, Destiny?"

"It's about the kids."

"What about the kids?"

"Montie, I'm moving to Miami. I mean, we are... me and the kids."

He sat his cup down and leaned against the counter. His lips clamped shut as he studied me. I assumed he was assessing whether I was serious or not. He walked over and took the seat in front of me and said, "I guess what the kids have been saying is true."

"The kids have been talking about moving?"

"Yeah, Montana talked about riding on a big plane and getting American Girl dolls. Junior was pumped about his game console. They told me Jacob took y'all to a big house down there and said you were moving into it. I thought they were just misinterpreting what they saw. Before now, I was one hundred percent sure you wouldn't do anything to cut me out of their lives. Moving them eight hundred miles away will definitely do that."

"It's true that Jacob wants us to move to Miami. He has already picked out our house and everything. But you will still be in their lives."

"Do you want to move to Miami?"

"To be with him, yes," I admitted.

Montie's tight expression fell. "So you're going to up and move my children to a different state where it will be damn near impossible for me to have any kind of meaningful relationship with them?"

"You will still be able to see them on your weekends."

"I never agreed to be a weekend father, Destiny. When we got divorced, I said from the jump I wanted to be active in my children's life. I'm not babysitting every now and then, we are co-parenting."

"I promise to fly them here every other weekend to see you, and the summers are still yours, Montie."

"That would probably work if you were dealing with the old me. It's not as simple as weekends and summers now. I go to Junior's football games and to the school for Father's Lunch Day. If Montana is sick, I'm on the list to pick her up from daycare. I'm an all-around dad. Ever since I realized what was most important in my life, I have been there for my kids and now you want to take that away."

"That is the last thing I want to do. I will keep you updated on any sport Junior is playing and you are welcome to use Jacob's private jet to travel back and forth between Atlanta and Miami so you can be present for games. And we can always use Skype."

"I don't want to talk to my kids over the damn phone, and I damn sho' can't eat lunch with them over Skype. As far as Jacob's jet, I don't need to use his shit. I need my kids to be in the same city as I am. It seems like you're trying to take them away and start over with a new father. They already have a father, Destiny."

"I am fully aware of who their father is."

"Are you?" Montie said with a raised brow.

"Of course, and I know this arrangement is not going to be perfect. But we can make this work, Montie."

He stared at me for a long time without saying anything, until he shook his head in disbelief. "What did I do to deserve this? All I did was try to love you and my children. Am I that bad of a person that you have to move my kids so far away?" he asked.

"My decision to move to Miami has nothing to do with you. It has everything to do with..." I paused before stating my reason. It was obvious my love for Jacob was strong enough to move to another continent, if that's where he wanted to go, but for some reason I couldn't say it to Montie.

"It has everything to do with being where Jacob will be. I get it. And if it were just you, I would have no problem with it. These are my children you're talking about moving away with, Destiny."

"And we are indeed moving. Of course, I want your blessing but I'm moving as soon as summer break starts. They will stay with you while I get settled, but once summer break is over I'll be back for them."

"What if I don't agree with your terms?"

"If we need to go to court to get this settled, then so be it."

Montie peered at me before he walked out of the room. "I'm going to get the kids' bags." When he brought the bags back, he handed them to me and then walked over and said goodbye to the kids. "I'll see you guys next week," he said hugging each of their necks.

Junior hugged him back and Montana placed a sloppy kiss on his cheek. "Lub you, daddy," she said before picking up her dolls and walking to the door.

This conversation was yet another finality in my relationship with Montie. Moving to Miami would not only place physical distance between us, it would put me on Jacob's terrain. Terrain I was ready to navigate with Montie's support or not.

Chapter 8

John

More Than a Side Piece

When I got back home, my feelings were even stronger than they were before I went to Atlanta. After having a heart-to-heart with Clara, I finally understood why I had carried around this underlying feeling of incompletion. The news of my lost child pummeled me in the chest every time I imagined marrying a young Clara with a rounded belly, carrying my child.

I never imagined my seed had been planted during our passionate moments. What if she'd bore my child — a beautiful, mixture of her bronze beauty and my ivory tone? Just thinking about the possibilities made it even more prudent that I did whatever necessary to make things right with her. I owed her the world and more for the pain I caused.

Had my visit gone the way I wanted it to? No. I knew from the start Clara would be a tough cookie to crumble. She was no nonsense, as she should've been. Stepping back into her world would take time and determination, and as a retired man of means I definitely had both.

I left shortly after breakfast feeling hopeful. I'd managed to make her crack one small smile by calling her Joanie, a pet name I had given her back in college. I always said she looked like a black version of the star on *Happy Days,* so I'd call her Joanie and she would instantly smile.

Her wonderful smile was still imprinted in my mind that evening. I sat in my home office thinking of ways to make that pretty smile happen again, until Tammy walked and interrupted my reverie.

"John?" she said in a low, sultry voice.

"What do you need, Tammy?" I asked without looking up.

"I need you, John."

Tammy's attempt at sounding ultra-sexy caused me to look in her direction. She was wearing a long, red gown with feathers around the collar and arms. Her red hair was straight and flowing down her shoulders and back. She had on a fair amount of makeup and bright red lipstick.

Her Botox-injected rosy cheeks rose into a phony looking smile, and she began unbuttoning her gown one button at a time. She attempted to seduce me with her eyes as each button popped open. When she reached the last button, she allowed the gown to slip down her body and to the floor. Underneath was a skimpy negligee, one like I'd never seen Tammy wear before.

Her body was that of an aged athlete, toned and shapely. There were also faint markings of the plastic surgeries Tammy had done to maintain the firmness in areas that would be otherwise sagging. If I said she wasn't beautiful standing there in her negligee, it would have been a lie.

"Tammy, you got yourself all dolled up for bed, I see. I was just about to head to bed too," I said, once I shook my attention from her body.

"I was hoping you could come up and sleep with me tonight. It's been over a year since we slept together. What do you say?" she asked as she played with the fabric around the neck of her nightie.

"With our divorce impending, I don't think that's a good idea."

I gave her a nod, hoping she would understand I wasn't interested in satisfying her sudden need to have me in our old bedroom.

"We need to reconnect on a deeper level, John. It's been a while since we've done that, and I think the lack of passion is what's driving you away," she said.

"Is that what you think?"

"Let me show you what I think," Tammy said as she began to sashay toward my desk. Her hand traveled to her rotund breasts and she began to rub the fabric above her round nipple. Her pouty lips puckered as she waited for my reaction.

I swallowed the lump in my throat and said, "That definitely won't be happening tonight, Tammy."

"Oh, stop being a prude, John," she said with a hand on her hip.

It was almost laughable that the same woman who seemingly invented the word prude was calling me one.

"Go to your bedroom, Tammy."

"Is that an order?" she said with a wink.

"You know, this is laughable."

"John, will you please work with me here? I'm trying my best to bring some spice into our marriage. I think we need to, you know... and then maybe you'll feel better," she said before running her tongue across her thin, pretty lips.

"No, I don't know. What do I need, Tammy?" I asked, entertaining her sudden interest in my needs.

"You know..." Tammy looked away coyly. "Some sex."

I got out of my chair and walked toward the door.

"Thanks, but no thanks. At this point, I don't need or want anything you have to offer. I'm going to my bedroom, and you should go to yours," I said.

Every muscle in my body tensed when she rushed to stand in the middle of the doorway to block me from exiting.

"The other day, you said I couldn't even kiss you and that's how you knew our marriage was over. Let me prove myself to you tonight. Let me give you what you want, John. We *need* to do this. You need me and I need you!"

"Tammy, you have no idea of what I need," I said as I stood inches away from her, looking into her eyes.

"Let me prove that I do," she pleaded. "Please let me prove it tonight."

"There is no way you can *prove* your love tonight. The proof is in the pudding. You have shown me, over and over again, where your heart is and it's not with me. You have put other people's feelings ahead of our family. You have disrespected this house, the business I run, and the people in both."

"John, you make it seem like I'm such a terrible person when I'm not. My family is first in everything that I do. I have given my entire life to my family."

"I noticed you purchased a pool house warming gift for the pool house the Parkers built. Since you put your family first, what have you bought for Jacob's new home that he purchased for his new family?"

"I haven't found the right thing..." she said, trying hard not to look bothered by my question. "I just haven't found it yet. That's all."

"Yet, you put all the staff on the task of finding a three-diamond soap dispenser for the Parker's shower that matched their décor to the letter?"

"I'll find something for Jacob's house tomorrow. I promise."

"Don't do it on my account, Tammy," I said, growing tired of the song and dance I had to do with her every time we saw each other since I informed her of the divorce.

"I was waiting to see what color schemes they chose before purchasing something, but I will definitely be getting a gift for my son's new home," she said, walking toward me and taking my hand.

"And this," I said making note of the lingerie she was wearing. "Miraculously, you own lingerie, when you have never worn anything as sexy in your life. In fact, you denied me nights like the one you're promising tonight more times than I can count."

I attempted to walk around her, but she rushed back to the door and blocked the way again. Her hands were on either side of the frame. "John, please just spend the night with me."

"No," I said firmly.

"Why are you doing this John?"

"I'm going to tell you this only once more, Tammy. It is over for us. If you don't stay out of my way while you're looking for a place to live, you're going to have to find a temporary place to stay until our divorce is final. This house is big enough that we don't even have to see each other, and that's what I prefer."

"This is as much my house as it is yours. I go where I want in it. If I see you, then so be it," Tammy said, pointing her finger into my chest.

"Well, just know I don't give idle threats. You keep pressing and I will show you whose house it really is." I gave her a look that brooked no argument.

I didn't like being so straightforward with her, but Tammy was the type that had to be handled frankly. I wanted to be clear that there would be no rekindling of our marriage. Who in their right mind would we rekindle something so miserable? With all the wasted years and all the damage that was done. I couldn't think of one thing worth rekindling.

"You will pay handsomely for the way you are treating me, John," she said turning around and walking away with her shoulders slumped in defeat.

"I already have paid, Tammy," I replied as I flipped the light switch off and walked down the long hall to my bedroom.

With these type of run-ins, our divorce being finalized couldn't come fast enough. Had Tammy shown me this type of attention a month ago, I would have devoured her where she stood in my study tonight. But at this point, all I wanted to do was make Clara Baker smile again. When I lay down in bed, I called her number.

"Clara?" I said, happy to hear her voice on the other end of the phone.

"What do you want, John? And who gave you my number?" she asked.

"I know you don't think I can get your address, but I can't get your number," I said on a laugh. "How I got the number is not important. What's important is me hearing your voice before I go to sleep tonight."

"Well, you need to go and hear your wife's voice."

"It's you that I want to talk to," I said.

"Listen, just because I gave you a hot meal and a few laughs doesn't mean you can start ringing my phone every time I turn around and you're definitely not allowed to pop up like you did this morning."

"That's what I was calling for. I want to know when I can see you again."

"Oh, let's see. How about when we enter the pearly gates of Heaven?"

"I'm serious, Joanie, I want to see you again."

"Stop calling me that stupid name. You lost the right to call me anything other than Ms. Clara Baker a long time ago."

"Come on, Clara, I know you don't want me to leave you alone any more than I want to."

There was silence for a short while. "I just don't see no sense in us unearthing old passions and hurts. Sometimes, it's just best to let sleeping dogs lie, John."

"Just see me one more time," I said, knowing full well I had no intention to ever let up.

"We don't have a reason to see each other again. I want you to go back to living your life like you were before that dinner and I will do the same."

"I can't do that."

"John, you don't have a choice this time around. You made your choice in nineteen seventy two and I'm going to make sure you continue to live by it."

"Nineteen seventy two. That was so many moons ago," I said as I blew out a deep breath. "I was young and very impressionable."

"Yes, you were," Clara agreed.

"I loved my grandfather a lot and I always respected what he worked for."

"What he built was admirable," she agreed again.

"I felt obligated to run our family's business, and my father was adamant I couldn't run the business with a black woman on my arm," I admitted.

"So you chose what was important and that was to run your family business. And from what I've read in the papers over the years, you have done well by that business. Why is it that you feel the need to come back in my life now, when our fate was sealed by your choice? "

"Knowing what I know now, I would never have chosen Turner Enterprises over you," I said, feeling the pain as the words left my lips. "However, I won't take all the blame. You could have told me you were pregnant."

"Well, John, life is all about choices. You chose your family business and I chose not to tell you about the baby growing inside of me. You fulfilled your obligations and I dealt with the consequences of our love affair alone. We both persevered through the challenges we faced and we both ended up here, separate. We made and lived with our choices, so I see no reason to change things up."

"We can chose a different path, now that we know better."

"Since you don't seem to be understanding the words coming out my mouth, let me tell you one thing!" she began yelling, before I cut her off.

"Oh, Clara, do you have to talk to me so rough? Where is the sweet, young girl I met at Wellmington? I know she's in there. Let me have her back."

"That sweet little girl is sixty five years old now! You act like you don't know how many years have gone by."

"I do know, I just... I don't know," I digressed.

"I have come terms with the fact that I will grow old alone. I even picked out the perfect rocker for me to sit on my front porch and crochet. I'm going to buy me a cute, little kitten and hang out all day with my animals, yarn patterns, and grandkids. What will not happen is you coming into my golden years and trying to make me a side piece.”

“What do you mean, side piece?”

“I mean, I wasn’t good enough to marry and move into your great big mansion, so I’m not good enough for you to fly in on your fancy jet in the middle of the day to fulfill whatever you’re trying to fulfill. I will not be your woman on the side.”

“I understand your distrust, but I would never make you a woman on the side, Clara. You have always deserved more and I promise to show you more. You just have to give me another chance.” There was silence on the other end, so I continued, “You don’t have to answer me tonight, just know I’m going to do whatever it takes to get you back.”

“Good night,” she said hanging up the phone before I could reply. Between Tammy’s display earlier and Clara’s ambivalence, I knew I had to speed up this divorce. I was ready to move into the next phase of my life.

Chapter 9

John

Invisible Lines

I coordinated with a local Atlanta flower delivery company to deliver forty fresh roses to Clara's home every day at 10:06 a.m. That time was sentimental. It was precisely the time I first laid eyes on her in the registration line at Wellmington. Before the deliveries would arrive each morning, I called her just to say, "Today is the beginning of the rest of our lives."

I hung up the phone immediately after staying those words for the first three days, but on day four she caught me. "John, don't hang up," she said, upon hearing my voice.

"How are you, Clara?" I asked.

"I'm doing really well. How about you?" she asked and I could almost hear the beam in her tone.

"Good, now that I'm talking to you," I replied, giving her my full attention. We went on to talk for a few minutes and she agreed to finally let me come see her again.

"When do you plan to come back to Atlanta?" she asked.

"I can be there today, if you want me there."

"Just whenever you're headed this way. No need to make a special trip," she said.

"Okay, I will talk to you soon, love," I said before hanging up the phone.

By noon, I was knocking on her front door. A beautiful aura surrounded Clara, when she opened the door. She stood in the midst of the assortment of colorful roses wearing a fitted coral dress and matching sandals. Her smile was glowing, which caused me to smile. I liked seeing her in such a good mood. I planned to make her smile like this every day for the rest of her life.

"I'm glad you kept the flowers," I said, making note of the colorful array of roses scattered about her setting room. Even though the room was filled with lovely sentiments, it still wasn't enough. She deserved a dozen for each moment of the day.

Clara looked around the room in shared amazement. "John, you didn't have to send me so many flowers. I almost don't have any space for them. There are so many flowers in here, I could start a flower shop."

"A thousand dozen wouldn't be enough for you. Besides, I see a little space where a few more could go," I said, pointing to an empty space on a table in the corner of the room.

She laughed. "Well, I'm not going to have any place to sit if you keep sending me flowers."

"That just means I'll have to get you a bigger house to hold them all," I said jokingly.

"There is not a thing wrong with my house, Mister."

I looked around at her timeless furniture. Some items I was sure she had since the seventies, others held memories of the decades passed by. There was a picture of her parents on the wall and a large framed photo of Dr. Martin Luther King adorning the wall's center.

"You're right, your home is lovely... just like you."

"Thanks," she said as she blushed. "I've been living in this old place since Destiny was born. I never really thought about leaving."

"Mind if I sit down?"

She nodded and I took comfort in the Victorian chaise close to the front door. It was then that I took in fully what she'd just said. She never really thought about leaving her home, which held memories that were near and dear to her heart. She had the courage to be still, when I was sure she could have done a million other things with her life. Her home was small and simple, yet extremely elegant. Every square foot held meaning that complimented her as a woman. A woman I admired from where I sat.

An overwhelming urge came over me, even stronger than I had the last time I was in her house. I wanted to wrap my arms around her and never let go. But I stayed seated, lest I upset her again.

"Can I get you something to drink, John? Water, iced tea, or something?"

"I'd like a glass of tea," I said, clearing the huge lump in my throat.

Lord have mercy, I thought, feeling like a fish out of water. Watching Clara walk away in that fitted dress and heeled sandals was a sight to behold. Her rotund rump looked as firm as I remembered it. I struggled to keep dragon raging within me at bay.

I wanted to follow Clara in that kitchen and demand we make up for missed time. But who was I kidding? Clara Santana Baker would surely roast me for dinner, if I crossed that invisible line.

"Here you are, John," Clara was saying when she reentered the room with two glasses of tea.

"Thank you." I took one glass from her hand and took a swig.

I scanned the many pictures lining her walls and adorning her winding bookcase. "You don't look a day older than you did in your twenties," I said, returning my attention to Clara to admire her unfading glow.

"Oh, John," she said as she sat down on the sofa beside me. "Don't try to get fresh with me. I look sixty plus and I'm glad about it."

I sat my glass down on one of the coasters she put on the coffee table. I took her drink out of her hand and sat it down, as well. I took both of her hands and just looked at her for a long while. I felt like that wet behind the ear chap that didn't know anything about love or life.

"You are so beautiful to me," I said as I eased closer to her on the sofa. "You are the most beautiful woman I have ever laid my eyes on."

She opened her mouth to speak and I sensed she was about to challenge me in some sort of way. It didn't matter what she was about to say; I didn't want to hear any of it. She was truly the most beautiful piece of artwork that graced this earth and I hoped she knew it. I moved in closer to her until our lips were but an inch away.

"I'm sorry for ever mistreating you," I said before taking a chance and moving in. I latched my lips to hers for a savory kiss. Her sweet, soft lips brought back distant memories of her soft and supple body being pressed up against mine, which aroused every part of me.

I was glad she didn't resist when I reached up and cupped her face. I captured the very essence of our kiss by holding her face in my hands. I held her within my own hands as I would a framed piece of artwork. The slow and sweet grinding of our lips progressed into a fiery, ferocious assault.

When I felt my loins harden to an epic proportion, I knew I had to release her, lest I made a mess of our reunion. There was no way I could control my hunger for her, if we continued this wonderful tease.

Just as I withdrew my lips from hers, she moaned. A sensuous moan that made me want to devour her whole. I wrapped my arms around her waist and damn near yanked her onto my lap. "You feel so good," I said moving my lips from her mouth to her neck.

"Umph... Oh, John, Mmmm... John," she said kissing me passionately. "I think we should stop..."

"Oh you feel so good, Clara," I said as my hands went on a quest to leave no part of her untouched.

"Stop, John... Stop it!" she said jumping out of my lap.

When she stood in front of me with accusing eyes, I knew it... I went too far. "Sorry, Clara. It just felt so good to kiss you again. I won't do it..."

"Damn it, John. Why did you have to come back here?" Clara asked as she straddled me and pulled my tie to guide my lips up toward to hers.

"I missed you," I murmured against her lips.

"How much did you miss me?" she asked, as she pushed me hard against the sofa.

"So much, words can't even explain," I said, as my back fell helplessly against the cushion.

I watched her every move, as she kicked off her shoes and slightly lifted her dress on each side. Her warm body encompassed my lap and her eyes demanded a real explanation as to how much I missed her. With my arms wrapped tightly around her waist, I pulled her down against my hardness. I kissed her with fever flowing from my lips to hers.

God, I'd forgotten what unbridled passion felt like. I wanted Clara so badly I didn't know how to contain myself. I pulled the straps of her dress down so I could lick the fabric of her black bra. My free hand slid up her dress and down into her silk panties. I cupped her bottom in my hands, just as her body went limp against mine.

When her moans ceased and she stopped moving, no words needed to be spoken. Our bad blood had come back like a thief in the night and overshadowed the moment.

Broken promises snuck in and reminded us both that I'd broken her heart. I removed my hand from her panties and straightened her dress back out. I eased the straps back up on her beautiful bronze shoulders. I pushed a few disheveled strands of her hair back in place and smiled at her in earnest.

"John, I'm sorry," she said faintly.

"Shhhhhh," I said placing a finger to her lips.

"I thought I was ready, but I'm just not ready for all of this," Clara said as she slid off my lap and sat beside me.

"Say no more," I told her as I put an arm around her and held her close.

In fairness, I never thought it would be as easy as a cup of tea, a sweet kiss, and a romp in the sack. I intended to be there for the long haul, to do whatever it took to get Clara's mind and heart back in the right place, with me.

We sat beside each other for a long while without saying a word. I would've given anything to kiss her sweet lips again, but nothing compared to knowing she still burned for me the same way I did for her. That was enough for me.

Chapter 10

Jacob

Love Lessons

"Hey, Dad, how are you?" I asked as I artfully held the phone to my ear. I walked into my new master bedroom with a box labeled 'master room.' I placed the box on top of a stack of boxes.

"I'm doing good, just feeling a little tired. I'll be by the office later today for my weekly review," Dad said on a yawn.

"Okay, I put all the files on your desk and emailed them to you, as well."

"Very good, Son. Last week's statements looked amazing. New business is up twenty percent in the Wyoming office and thirty three percent in the Delaware office. You were definitely on to something with those two offices," he said with pride.

"Yeah, I felt pretty strong about the potential in those two places. It's only right that Turner Enterprises has a footing in every state in America. I'm confident Delaware and Wyoming will continue to carry their own weight and eventually show exponential growth," I said, taking the phone off speaker.

"Well, you don't have to sell it to me anymore. The proof is in the numbers," Dad said.

"Dad, I have something personal to ask you."

"What's on your mind, Son?"

"When Destiny talked to Ms. Clara this morning, she said you were at her house last night. Is that true?"

"Yes, we were together. Why?"

"I just didn't know things were getting serious enough for you to spend the night at her house." I guess in the back of my mind I was holding out some hope that my parents could reconcile.

"If you must know, Clara and I sat and talked about the good times we shared. We laughed and talked until about twelve in the morning. Then, I flew back to Miami and stayed in a hotel. Your mother has been crowding me and I needed some space to think."

"So you didn't spend the night with Ms. Clara?"

"No, I stayed at a hotel. Is that okay with you Son, or do I have a curfew?" Dad asked sarcastically.

"You don't have to report to me. I'm just looking out for our family."

"Rest assured that no one has looked out for our family more than me. I have the wounds on my heart to prove it. I won't do anything to damage our family any more than it already is, but I am going to be happy, which brings me to the reason I called. Have you heard from your mother?"

"I haven't talked to her in a few days, why?"

"When I got home this morning, she wasn't here and her room had been cleared out. The staff said the movers came by early this morning and packed her up."

"She didn't tell me she was moving out. Did she leave a note or anything?" I asked.

"Nothing. My first thought is that she got the condo she's been talking about. It's interesting that she didn't tell you anything or leave word for me."

"When I last spoke to her, she had come to the conclusion that she would move on. But I don't like her making moves like this without talking to someone. I don't want her to feel like she has to be alone, when she has a son who cares about her," I said, feeling some type of way.

"Even though we're getting a divorce, I still care about her wellbeing too. That's why I called."

"Yeah, I know you do," I said absentmindedly. "I'll call around and check on her in just a little while," I added while studying the various items scattered about my bedroom.

I walked over to stand in the doorway of the walk-in closet and stared at Destiny who was removing items from a box and placing them on the shelves. She had given the delivery guys the okay to leave without unpacking all of our things, after I explicitly told her to make sure they unpacked everything down to the last garment. I shook my head at her defiance.

"Well, listen, you sound busy, so I'll just talk to you later," Dad said. "Tell Destiny I said hello."

"Sure thing," I said as I hung up the phone. I walked back into the bedroom and called out for Destiny. She had been moving around like a little mouse all day, organizing this and cleaning that. The way she was carrying on, one would never imagine that we had a full staff to assist her.

"Yes, babe," she said as she entered the bedroom.

"First of all, what is all this stuff in these boxes?"

"Our things that came from Atlanta," she said.

"I thought the movers were supposed to unpack everything and put it in the correct place.

Will you explain to me why we have boxes that still have items in them?" I asked. The clutter was actually beginning to wreck my nerves.

I grabbed the box she was unpacking and placed it on the bed. I motioned around the room at all of the boxes. I was finding out that she had a compulsion to do everything herself, which was why we were left with a full house to unpack.

"I told them we could handle it. I wanted to put everything up, so I know where it is and to make sure it's put up correctly," she said with a shrug.

"Oh, so you just told them you would unpack an entire mansion by yourself?"

"With your help…"

"Oh, no! I'm not unpacking any of this, especially after I told you to have the movers do it. Is this your idea of being a submissive wife?"

"Jacob…" she said with her mouth dropping open. "I know you're not upset about me unpacking."

"I'm not upset with you for packing. However, I paid the movers to do the job you're doing. I'm about to call them back, so they can get over here and finish doing the job I paid them to do. And you're going to let them do their job."

"Jacob, you can't be serious," she pouted.

"I'm very serious," I told her as I walked toward her.

"But it would be cool if we spent time together fixing our house up just the way we want it. I thought you said you took the rest of the week off."

"It will be the way we want it. We're just not going to be the ones doing it. I took the week off, but I'm not going to spend it unpacking." Our newly hired maid, Lynetta, passed by the doorway as I thumped a box on the bed. She was carrying a box as well. I called out to her, "Lynetta, will you come in here for a second?"

"Yes, Mr. Turner," Lynetta said coming back to stand just outside the door.

"Come on in," I ordered, and she walked into the room. "As the head of maid services, maybe you can explain to me why my fiancé is in here working like she's on the staff."

"Sir, Ms. Destiny said she would..."

I cut her off. "Destiny is not to lift a finger unpacking these boxes, regardless of what she says. I want you to place a call to the movers and get them back over here so they can finish unpacking the things that came from our houses in Atlanta. As well, I want you to personally direct them while they are getting this task done. Don't let them leave here until everything is in its place. And tell them to send the invoice for any extra hours and I'll get it taken care of. Is that clear?"

Lynetta nodded her head. "Yes, sir, boss. I will call them back immediately," she said making note of what she was to do. She glanced at Destiny before rushing off to make the call.

"As for you," I said, pushing our door closed. "You can make this easy on yourself or you can make it hard. Either way, it's going to be fun for me," I added.

"What are you talking about, Jacob?" Destiny asked.

"There are a list of things I want my wife doing with her day and manual labor is not on the list."

"Oh, yeah? I guess now is a good time for you to fill me in on what's acceptable for me to do in a day and what's not," Destiny said with a slight attitude.

"Well, you could always work on one of your ad campaigns," I began, pushing the box from the bed and pushing her down onto the bed. I took my time in admiring her beauty. "But for starters, you can work on staying stunningly sexy, so I can look at you like this."

Destiny leaned forward on her elbows. "Is that all what you want, Mr. Turner? For me to be the object of your desires... to spend my days with my only goal being to look beautiful for you?" Destiny asked as she looked up at me with questions in her eyes.

"That and of course this, too," I said as I bent down to lick her lips before prying her mouth open for a kiss.

"Mmmh," she said as her spirit blended with mine over a sensual kiss. "So, Mr. Turner, you basically want me to lay in this bed looking sexy and to be ready for your kiss at all times?"

I sprinkled kisses all over her face before answering, "Yes."

"I think I can do that."

"Your new job description as my wife is to wake up, get sexy, and be ready for me to have my way with you."

"What if I want to apply for something more challenging?" she asked as her legs spread wide and then wrapped around my back.

"You are a well-qualified applicant, so I'm confident you can handle this position and added duties that might be thrown your way."

"No matter how hard it is?" she asked, gripping my manhood in her hands.

"It will be very hard, but in the highly unlikely chance that you can't handle it," I said as I pressed my hands against each of her legs and pressed them against the bed. "You'll receive disciplinary action."

"Like punishment?"

"Yeah, consider this your first oral reprimand," I said as I unbuttoned her jeans and yanked them down her legs. Kissing the material of her panties as I went down her body, I removed her panties with my teeth in a swift motion and shoved my tongue into her heat. My tongue flicked over her bud in earnest, until she gripped the covers underneath her.

"Mmmh, you taste so good," I said before sucking her clit into my mouth. My head moved up and down her canal as my tongue became one with her sweet body. I didn't let her go until she was trembling. Then, I picked her up and playfully tossed her onto the middle of our fluffy bed. Tremors were still moving through her body as I unbuckled my pants and stepped out of them.

"I think I like getting in trouble," she said as she recovered.

I climbed up onto the bed and rubbed my hardness. "Show me that you understand your oral reprimand," I said as I stroked the heaviness in my hand. "What I just told you, run it back for me."

She climbed up on all fours and inched toward me. When her tongue touched the tip of my dick, chills shot through my body. She licked from the tip to my shaft and then took me into her mouth.

"I like the way you relay information," I said as I thrust into her mouth as she opened up to receive me. I plunged into her warm, wet mouth with long thrusts. She gripped my shaft and received my relentless strokes, until I threw my head back and said, "I'm coming. Ugh!"

My hot cum spewed out over her lips and she licked it into her mouth. She lay down on her back and began massaging her lower lips. There was no way I could reach organic heaven without taking her to the hilt, as well. With my member still hard, I mounted her and dove in.

She was hot and ready to succumb to the mounting pleasure. Surprisingly, it was a struggle to hold my composure as I began my verbal lesson, "Tell Lynetta what you need her to do. Do you understand?" Each time I said a word I rammed into her pussy good, causing her to jolt back onto the bed. I made sure every inch of my dick filled her with each syllable.

"Yes, I understand," she submitted with ease.

"We have much better things to do with our time than unpack. Do you understand?"

"I understand! I will let Lynetta do it, I promise," she said as her body began to quiver uncontrollably.

Satisfied that she saw things my way, I knew I was going to enjoy teaching her many more lessons about being my wife. “I want you to have my baby. Do you understand?” I said as I rammed into her heat over and over.

“Yes! I understand. Put your babies inside of me. Give me your babies, Jacob!” Destiny said as she met my stroke for stroke. When her good pussy gripped my shaft so tight that I felt like she was pulling the life right out of my body, I came hard, once again filling her with my seed.

I didn’t dare move. I lay on top of her and allowed her warmth to encompass my body. I pulled her as close to me as she could possibly get in order to allow every seed from my body to enter hers in hopes that she would soon carry my child.

As I lay there in Destiny's warmth, the thought of my baby growing in her womb caused me to instantly harden again. Destiny stirred beneath me and moaned. Her tongue licked the sweat from my chest. The feel of her soft tongue against my chest set fire to the dying embers as it stirred my insatiable thirst for the woman I loved more than any other.

"Jacob," Destiny gasped beneath me. "I can't seem to get enough of you.”

"The same is for me, sweet Destiny," I admitted as I began to stir in her once again.

Her core gladly received me as her walls pulsated around my hardness. I grew stiffer and stiffer inside her heat...like granite.

How is this even possible? I silently questioned the way my body responded like never before. Our bodies grew slicker and slicker against each other as the slapping sounds of our passion filled the room like music. We danced to our own rhythm.

"Fuck me, Jacob," Destiny threw her hips upward to meet each of my downward thrusts. I lifted one if her thighs higher in the air to I penetrate her deeper. The deeper I plunged into Destiny's heat, the deeper I tried to embed myself into her soul. A thunderous sound of my heartbeat exploded in my ears as I neared completion.

"Oh, my God, Jacob, I'm cumming again," she said as she marked my back with her finger nails raking down my skin.

The sharp pain from her nails sent me into a frenzy and over the edge I went as my growls joined her sweet moans. I fucked her harder until our orgasms rocked us both to the core. Neither of us could move after our last round of intense lovemaking, but I somehow found the strength to rollover without disconnecting our bodies. Our breathing slowed to normal as we held each other in silence. The love we felt for one another spiked volumes in our moment of silence while luxuriating in our love.

*

Destiny emerged from our bathroom after showering and getting dressed an hour later. I had showered in the guest bathroom and slid into a pair of pajama bottoms and house shoes, while she was dressed to the nines in a purple dress and heeled sandals. Her well-oiled skin seemed to be calling my attention to its sweetness. I stood behind her at the mirror while she was combing her hair. "You must not want to make it out of this house coming out here dressed like that." I said.

"Stop kidding around," she said waving me away before adjusting her diamond necklace.

I snaked my arms around her waist. "You know I don't kid around about what I want."

"Jacob, I just got showered and got dressed," she pouted. "Plus, Tasha will be here to pick me up any minute."

"In that case, I guess you're saved by the bell," I said as the doorbell chimed through the house.

Within seconds, Lynetta's voice chimed through the intercom system. "Miss. Destiny, you have a guest. A Miss Tasha Baker."

"She'll be down in just a second," I said, spinning her around to kiss her lips before letting her go.

Instead of doing housework, I talked her into having some fun at the spa with Tasha. They also planned to spend some time going over the details of Montana's birthday party that was fast approaching.

Once Destiny swished her sweet tail out of our bedroom, I decided to call and check on my mother. "Hello, Mom… glad you answered," I said, when she answered on the second ring.

"Hi, Son, you called my number. Why wouldn't I answer?"

"Dad's been trying to get in touch with you today and you weren't answering your phone," I said with a question in my voice.

"Why would I answer the phone for him when he chooses to spend his time philandering with that woman?"

"I would hardly call what Dad is doing philandering, Mom."

"I don't expect you to take my side, Jacob. After all, you both are barking around the same trees."

"I didn't call for all this extra conversation. I just wanted to make sure my mother was still alive and well."

"Well, unfortunately I haven't croaked, so you and your father still have to deal with me," she said bluntly. I heard the sound of glass clanking and light music in the background. "I just walked into the restaurant to meet Martha and Janice, I'll call you soon, Jacob."

"Okay, I love you, Mom," I said.

Mom paused for a minute, as if she were thinking about her reply. "Same here, Jacob," she said before hanging up. She had been brief, but I was glad she was hanging with her friends. The last thing I wanted her to do was sit around and sulk over Dad.

Having sent my favorite girl on her way to a relaxing day and checked on my other favorite girl, I felt accomplished.

Chapter 11

Destiny

When the Caged Bird Swings

"I wish yo' ass would stop smiling all the damn time. You remind me of how single and celibate I am. Two things I loathe at the moment," Tasha said as we sat out on the patio at an eatery. The sun was shining through a few dubious clouds as we caught up on the planning for Montana's birthday party coming up in a month.

"Am I smiling? I didn't even know," I said, innocently.

"Bitch, you know your ass is cheesing like somebody bought crackers up in here. I know you're in love, but do you have to rub it in?"

"Damn, Tasha, the hate and shade is so real today. Are you PMSing?"

"I'm sorry, girl. Yes, I'm PMSing, horny, and everything else. Every dude I've met in the past two months ain't been about shit," she said taking a sip of her soda.

"Sounds like you're going through it, boo."

"It's just another day in the life of Tasha Baker," she said on a sigh. "How are you enjoying my city so far?"

"It's okay. A lot like Hotlanta in some ways with the heat, traffic, and people's attitudes. I love my new house though."

"I bet you do," Tasha said, taking another sip.

"I feel like a queen on a throne with people cooking dinner, unpacking, helping with this and that. You know me, I'm still used to doing a lot for myself, so all of this will take some getting used to."

Tasha shook her head and laughed. "If those are all the problems you have, I don't think you'll have a problem overcoming them."

"On that I must agree," I said as I picked up my glass and clacked it to hers. I then squeezed a piece of lemon into my tea, before sipping some of the heavenly fluid through my straw.

"I can't believe Montana is turning four already," Tasha said.

"Yep, and when I talked to her on the phone last week she was adamant that she wants a Doc McStuffins themed party. I'm cool with that and want to do something simple, but Jacob is intent on turning our backyard into Doc

McStuffins' own personal hospital, staff included."

"Girl, you know Jacob is extra."

"Exactly, he has gone so far as to contact Brown Bag Films to get copies of the original sketches so his assistant could get someone to craft life size costumes of Doc McStuffins and all of the other characters on the show. He's also ordered six hours of the original Doc McStuffins character for the party, as well."

"Owweee! Montana is going to be stoked. Hell, I'm stoked for her."

"I'm stoked, too. I just want my kids to stay grounded. That's going to be hard when they have everything they could ever want at their fingertips."

"Yeah, but you're grounded so your kids will be, too. Is Montie going to fly in on Jacob's jet with the kids?" Tasha asked with a suspicious looking grin.

"No, why do you ask?"

"Just wondering if he decided to take you up on the offer."

"He's adamant about booking flights and paying for it himself. He hasn't come around to the whole idea of using Jacob's jet for traveling back and forth between here and Atlanta."

"Can you blame the man?" Tasha asked.

"It would make things so much easier if he would just..."

"Listen to yourself, Destiny. Not very long ago, you were in the bed with Montie sending mixed signals about where you stood. Now, you want him to fly around on your fiancé's jet. Any man with a little bit of pride wouldn't do that."

"I guess you're right, since you put it that way."

"I'm just being real. It's not like you are that far from another romp in the sack."

"See that's where you're wrong. I would never do anything like that again. I was in a very vulnerable place then, and I fully intend not to let that history repeat," I said and I meant it from the depths of my soul.

"As long as you believe that and stay strong, it's possible," Tasha said trying to sound convincing. "I just know through your children you have a forever kind of bond and you never know when a situation might come up that makes you feel like he's the only one you can turn to."

"I will turn to the man God sent for me, Jacob. Montie will always hold a special place in my heart. He's the father of my children and will always be a friend."

"That's good."

"I'm just glad he didn't make a big deal about us moving."

"What made him come around?" Tasha asked.

"I was firm that it was happening whether he liked it or not. He's agreed to my ideas of ways to establish a long-distance relationship with our children, starting with Montana's birthday party. Technically, he could've kept her in Atlanta because summer break is his time."

"I'm glad he's being understanding. With you, Jacob, and Montie, Junior and Montana have more than some children will ever get in life. They are blessed," Tasha said with a smile. "By the way, have you run into any brothers, distant cousins, long lost uncles... any more good Turner men?"

"His father is the only other Turner man I've met, and he's pretty much smitten with Mama," I said as I continued to wrap my mind around the idea of my mother rekindling things with Jacob's father. "That, oddly enough, is about all I can deal with at the moment."

"Hell, it's not odd to me. Aunt Clara is just getting her payback and her groove back, that is all."

"Well, she needs to put her groove back where it was. I don't know how to feel about her hooking up with Jacob's father."

"When I called her the other day, she sounded like an angel on the phone. I should have known something was up. She was so pleasant that I almost hung up and redialed the number. I was sure I had the wrong house. It's a change for the better."

"This is definitely a change for Mama," I said, just as a group of older women approached our table. I didn't pay them much attention, until the lady bringing it up the rear spoke and I recognized who she was.

"That's the home wrecker's daughter right there," Mrs. Tammy Turner said. She was walking with Martha Parker, who was Justine's mother, and another woman wearing a hideous floral pantsuit.

"Humph, if that's her offspring, don't look like he left you for much," the woman in the floral suit said as she turned up her snoot.

"Excuse me?" I stood up and asked. I could take disrespect. But there was no way I could stay seated while these old biddies talked about Mama.

"I was speaking to my friend, not to you Pestiny... Ooops, I mean Destiny," Mrs. Turner said as her evil eyes glared straight through me.

"See, this is that shit that get folks fucked up," Tasha said, standing beside me and taking off her earrings. "I was trying to turn down, but you bitches bout to get it."

"Oh, and I assume your foul mouth is supposed to scare me," Mrs. Turner said, feigning fear by clutching her chest.

"Mrs. Turner, we were not bothering you. You were talking about me and my mother, and that's the only reason I even addressed you," I said, without addressing the name slight.

"I most absolutely was talking about you and I'm pretty sure you heard what I said. Your mother is a home wrecker," Mrs. Turner said. "I was reading somewhere that you young people call what your mother is doing something specific these days. What was it? Oh, thirsty... that's it, thirsty," she said with a snap of her fingers. "And what is this other word you people use? Oh yeah, thot is the word I am looking for. Yo' mama is a thot," she said in slang.

Martha and the other woman laughed, both repeating, "thirsty... thot," as they cracked up beyond control. "And from what I heard, the apple don't fall too far from the tree," Martha added as their laughter died down.

"Mrs. Parker, you have no room to talk about how far an apple falls from a tree when you have raised Justine, one of the most violent, narcissistic psychopaths of this century." I turned my attention back to Mrs. Turner. "And my heart goes out to you. Not because you are losing your husband, but because you are too stupid to understand why."

"Why, I'm sure that you, Destiny, with your high level of intelligence, could enlighten me as to what John sees in your mother. Whatever it is I can't see it with my eyes."

"You'll have to ask him what he sees in her. However, she wouldn't have been able to come into your home and wreck anything, if your marriage wasn't already broken," I said.

"Is that what you people think, that my marriage was broken?" she asked stepping closer to me. "I'll have you to know I made John a very happy man over the years and I continue to make him happy. He's never complained before and he's still not complaining," Mrs. Turner raised her eyebrow as if her words had a double meaning.

"You would think a woman your mother's age would have more respect for a woman's husband, but then again I don't expect much from your kind," the lady in the floral pantsuit said.

"They both are just trying to find a way to get a part of the Turner fortune," Martha said.

"Well, guess what? That will be over my dead body," Mrs. Turner said.

"I don't see a problem with that!" Tasha said, with her dinner fork in hand. "Destiny might take kindly to you standing over our table talking shit about her and my aunt, but I don't. You and your little posse better clack your heels on these bricks and get your asses out of our faces before this becomes a 911 situation."

The lady wearing the floral gasped, while Martha took Mrs. Turner's hand and pulled her along. "I'm not scared of her," Mrs. Turner said once they were a few feet away. "If she touches one hair on my body, I will have her hauled away for the rest of her pathetic life."

I followed her saying, "Mrs. Turner, I love your son and I have nothing to do with what happened in my mother's past. I've tried to be respectful to you. Lord knows, I really have. But you're making it nearly impossible to have even a cordial relationship with you. I think we both should try to at least be cordial, for Jacob."

"Even if your tramp of a mother wasn't trying to steal my husband, I never would've liked you. Jacob and John may think it's fine to pick up strays, but I will never play in the hay with you, little girl. I don't approve of my son stooping to the level of marrying you. I hope he comes to his senses before it's too late. After this conversation, I want you to be clear on how I feel about you, so that you will never, ever attempt to talk to me again."

"Fuck you!" I said as my mind went black. "Fuck you!" My hand reared back and slapped Mrs. Turner so hard that her entire left face immediately filled with raging blood vessels. "I'm not an animal and my mother is not a tramp!" I said as I spat in Mrs. Turner's face, before swinging at her again.

"Oh, my God," Martha said as she frantically took out her cell phone to call 911.

"Come here, bitch!" Tasha said, grabbing Martha by the arm and yanking her cell phone out of her hand. She threw it to the ground and stepped on it. "All of you disrespectful hoes are about to get what you deserve."

"You have no right to step on her phone," the lady in the floral suit said as she swung her purse and hit Tasha in the face.

Tasha pushed the lady away from her and the lady tripped over a chair and fell to the ground landing on her ass.

"My word, you black people really are animals," Martha said, rushing to the door and yelling for help. "Somebody help! My friends and I are being attacked."

By that time, the restaurant's management team came onto the patio with two husky men. I was regaining my self-control, while searching for my dignity in the situation, when one of the men grabbed me and held me against the wall.

"What's going on?" the restaurant manager asked.

"That one. She hit me and spit on me," Mrs. Turner said pointing in my direction. The smug look on her face let me know that I'd messed up.

"The police are on their way. I just called them," Martha said to the manager. She was holding her banged up phone in her hand as she looked at me with the same smugness as Mrs. Turner. Her chest heaved up and down as she added, "You tried to make my baby out to be a criminal. This time, they're going to take the real criminal to jail."

"The truth always rises to the top," Mrs. Turner added.

I looked at Mrs. Turner and her friends standing there playing the victim, while having low-key, shit-eating grins their faces. They seemed to be professionals as they feigned innocence and devastation to the manager.

It was going to be a long day. Hell, possibly even a long weekend in jail. I felt like crap for allowing them to take me so far out of character. I'd gone from crafting ideas for my daughter's birthday party in the backyard of my new mansion to facing jail time all in a matter of hours.

The manager was a young, white girl who looked to be no older than twenty. She looked at me as if she couldn't believe I'd hit and spit on an elderly woman. She walked over to me and asked, "Did you attack that woman?"

"After she stood over my table and insulted me and my mother, yes I did. I blacked out and didn't know what I was doing."

"I'm going to have to ask you to come with me until the police get here," she said in obvious disappointment.

Tasha and I were escorted into the manager's office, while Mrs. Turner and her crew rubbed their injuries and moaned in pain. I was in such shock over how quickly things happened. I didn't know what to expect, as I sat quietly waiting for the police to arrive.

"There's no doubt that these folks are going to take us to jail, so stop sitting there looking like a lump on a log and call Jacob," Tasha said.

"What do you want me to say? Hello, Jacob, I just slapped the shit out of your mother and my cousin beat up her friend, come bail me out?" I asked.

"First tell him how they disrespected us and then tell him you slapped the shit out of his mother and I beat up her friend. I really don't care how you break it to him, just tell him what's going on in case they try to take us to jail, Destiny."

"You think we're going to jail?" I asked Tasha.

"It's our word against theirs and from the looks of things," she said, looking around at the all-white management team who was carefully attending to Mrs. Turner and her friends. "Our word might not make it."

"Well, I did hit her. I shouldn't have done that."

"With the way she was talking to you, it's a wonder you didn't whoop her ass to sleep. I know I wanted to."

"No matter what she said, I shouldn't have done that Tasha. I feel terrible."

"Look, either call Jacob and tell him what happened or give me his number. We will need someone to come bail us out."

I wasn't prepared to call Jacob and tell him I'd slapped his mother, so I gave Tasha the number. She tried to reach him, but he didn't answer the phone. As she was about to leave a message, an officer arrived.

"Ma'am, I'm going to have to ask you to get off the phone," the officer said.

Tasha ended the call and put her phone in her purse. Then, after hearing our side of the story, the officer placed us both under arrest for assaulting Mrs. Turner and her friend. I didn't resist the arrest. I knew I was wrong for putting my hands on her.

"What exactly are we being arrested for?" Tasha asked as another officer put her hands behind her back.

"Assault and disorderly conduct," the officer said before reading us both our rights. Mrs. Turner was being attended to by a paramedic looking shining his penlight into her ear as we were escorted out of the restaurant.

"You look like a nice lady, but the victims want to press charges, so we have to take you both to the station," the officer escorting me out said.

Mrs. Turner smiled as I was being carted away to be locked in a cage, just like the animal she claimed I was. I was so pissed at myself for letting her win.

"We're going to get out of this," Tasha said once we were both in the back of the police car. "Just call Jacob as soon as they allow us to make a phone call."

"I thought called him already," I said through a shaky voice.

"They came in before I was able to leave a message."

"Okay, I'll call him when we get there. I know he will come and straighten this out."

It didn't really matter how the rest of the evening turned out. Just the mere satisfaction on

Mrs. Turner's face as I the police car pulled away from the curb with me and Tasha in the backseat caused me to ball in anger.

Tasha leaned into me so I could cry on her shoulder. The loud crackling of thunder followed by the first signs of drizzling rain matched my mood. I finally let the tears flow freely down my face.

Chapter 12

Jacob

A Brewing Storm

“Wanda, thanks for calling me with an update on the Smith account. Use my signature stamp to sign off on the necessary paperwork, and I’ll follow up to make sure everything is in order,” I told my secretary. She was quickly stepping up the bar from being a secretary to being an executive assistant. I never feared that business wasn’t getting handled when she was on the job. She was just that good.

“Sure, I will stamp any forms that require your signature. If anything looks out of order, I will give you a call,” Wanda said.

“Okay, what about that special project I had you working on?” I asked.

“Oh, I contacted Tom today and he agreed to meet with you. He sounded like he was ready to talk,” Wanda said of our old VP of Finance. I had some questions for him about others who may have been working with him inside the company when he embezzled millions of dollars a few months back. I was glad he was willing to talk. I wanted to make sure everyone involved had been weeded out.

"That is very good, Wanda, very good. Is there anything else I should know before I come back in Monday?" I asked, as I looked out my library window. The once bright sun was recoiling and dark clouds were covering any semblance of a beautiful day.

"That's it, boss. I will call you if anything comes up. In the meantime, enjoy your vacation days," Wanda said sounding cheerfully reassuring.

"Thanks for all you do, Wanda. I will definitely enjoy my time off," I said, hanging up the phone. Wanda had to be one of the highest paid secretaries in America, and she was worth every dime.

My next call was to Destiny, which went straight to voicemail. It wasn't like her not to answer her cell when she was out. I figured she was either driving home or in a location where her phone didn't have good service. Either way, she needed to hurry home, so I'd be able to keep her safe in this brewing storm.

As time passed, the drizzling rain turned into hard thumps against the windowpane. Worrisome, nasty clouds began to roar, causing mounting tension to build in my muscles. Knowing the other half of me was out in the midst of a storm did not settle well with my spirit.

After a few minutes passed, I called Destiny again and left a new message. When she didn't return my call on the next three tries, I activated the GPS locator on my phone to search for her location. If she was stuck out in this messy weather, I had to find her. After waiting a full minute for the tracker to scan for Destiny's location, the GPS locator proved useless. The only conclusion I could come to was that her phone was off or her battery was dead.

"Damn it, Destiny," I said, after dropping my cell down onto my desk. I sat down and tried to take my mind off her whereabouts. She was with Tasha, who knew Miami well, and more than likely she was just somewhere where her phone didn't receive good service. I hoped Tasha wouldn't try to drive if it got too bad out.

To occupy my mind, I sat behind my desk and concentrated on the proposal Destiny was putting together for the national ad campaign Turner Enterprises was about to undertake. I flipped through various text campaigns and visual ads, as well as the TV commercial that would be launching in the fall. It all looked exceptional and was slated to run over into the Super Bowl, with one major ad during the most epic football affair of the year.

I picked up my cell and called her once again, after looking at the last piece of media. Again, her phone went straight to voicemail. This time, I left a more urgent message. “Hey, babe, I hope everything is okay. It’s looking pretty bad out there. I need to hear your voice. When you get this message, call me immediately. Love you.”

I hung up the phone and sat down on my lounger. I racked my brain as to why Destiny wasn’t answering as I stared at the rain cascading down the window. The harder the rain fell the more worried I got. I rubbed my temples to release the building tension. “She’s with Tasha, and they’re okay,” I reminded myself again.

I rested my head on the pillow-top lounger, where I sat waiting for Destiny to return my call. As I lounged in the comfortable chair, I began to relax. Soon, I had drifted into a deep slumber. The house was completely dark, when I awoke hours later.

I rubbed my eyes and looked around the room. I couldn’t even see my hand in front of my face. I felt my way to the window and looked out into the pitch black night. The entire street was dark, not even a distant streetlight was in view. “Dang, there must be a power outage and the generator didn’t kick in,” I said remembering that setting the generator was still on my to-do list.

At that moment, I regretted letting Lynetta and her crew have the evening off once they unpacked the upstairs rooms. I was sure one of them would've thought to set the generator had they been there during the storm. Just as that thought crossed my mind, I heard footsteps and turned to see Destiny entering the room.

A bolt of lightning quickly flashed into the room and a glimmer of her shiny red negligee shined through the darkness. Her vanilla fragrance wafted through the room and caused me to smile. "Hey, babe, I'm glad you made it home safe," I said walking toward her.

She pressed a finger against my lips when I reached her. Gripping my face into her hands, she pulled me toward her for a kiss. As our kiss deepened, my arms made their way around her waist and I pulled her close. Just as quickly as I captured her, she stepped out of my embrace and poked her finger into my chest, pushing me toward the chaise.

I wanted her back in my arms, but I followed her lead. I fell down onto the chaise and waited for her to perform the sensual tease she started. "Oh, so this morning was just the preview for tonight, huh?" I asked as my hand rested on her thigh. I felt the fabric of her negligee travel down my arm, until it slid off and hit the floor.

She grinded her body against mine in quiet seduction as I sat on the edge of the chair. The house was so tranquil I could hear my heartbeat. I squeezed her thighs in anticipation of the pleasure I'd have once the silence was replaced by her moans filling the room. The thought of consecrating my library during this ugly storm had my loins on fire. The mysteriousness of the moment also added to my rambunctious drive for consummation.

She felt her way down my body until she reached my pants and then pulled them down as far as she could. I assisted her by adjusting in the chair. Once we were free of any barriers, she goofily straddled my lap. I wanted to suck her breasts, run my hands through her hair and caress her body. However, she intertwined her fingers with mine to keep me at bay and eased down onto my shaft.

Her wet, snug pussy meticulously devoured my manhood, inch by inch. I could feel her lose control of her tight muscles every time she rose and fell against me. I grabbed her waist and urgently guided her down my shaft. Whatever she'd done that day to tighten her body made her feel amazing.

I wanted to give as good as I was receiving, so I hugged her close and thrust into her repeatedly. "You feel so good," I told her, when my balls began to tingle. If I hadn't impregnated her already, this release would be a sure shot. My baby makers were ready and aiming for her heated core as I let go of every drop of passion in my soul.

"Oh, Jacob! I've waited for this moment for so long. I missed you so much," Justine said as she crashed down onto my dick one last time.

Her irritating voice caused my heart to drop into my stomach. However, the imminent orgasm traveling through my loins paralyzed me. It was too late. By the time I pushed her away, my explosion had already erupted deep inside her womb.

"Get the fuck off me!" I said pushing her down onto the floor.

"Aw, come on now, Jacob. Don't try to act like you didn't know it was me."

"I didn't... I mean, I couldn't have. I never would've let you touch me. I'm calling the fucking police, you sick bitch!" I said as I got up and put on my pants. I felt around for my cell that was on my desk.

"And tell them what? I just made love to my ex? Don't waste your time or the time of our police department. By the way your body responded to me, you missed me as much as I missed you. We belong together."

"I don't miss you, at all, Justine. I thought you were my wife."

"Keep telling yourself that."

By this time, I was pulling her by the arm toward the door. "Just when I thought you couldn't hit any lower, you hit rock bottom. What kind of lowlife sneaks into a man's house, puts on his wife's clothes and perfume, and pretends to be his wife?"

"Jacob, you can say what you want about me, but what you can't say is that you didn't enjoy every minute of being inside of me. The way you moaned and groaned told another story."

There was a beeping sound just as the lights came back on illuminating the room. I picked up Destiny's negligee and threw it at her. "Put this back on and get the hell out of my house."

"So now you want to treat me like a two-bit whore? Un uh, after what we just shared, you're going to have to deal with me and hopefully the baby growing in my stomach," Justine said as her hand fell to her stomach.

"Justine, unless you want me to escort you out of here naked, you'd better put that gown and get out of here. What clothes did you wear here? How in the hell did you get in here, anyway?" I asked wanting answers.

"Wouldn't you like to know?" she said as she angrily put on the negligee.

"I so tired of your shit, Justine. You are going to make me do something I will regret," I said, before picking up the phone and dialing 911. "I'm just calling the police before this gets out of hand and you get hurt."

"Go ahead, call them! But then, you'd have to admit to Destiny that you fucked me and liked it. You will have to explain how your sperm ended up in my womb. I'd love to be a fly on the wall for that conversation." She let out a cruel laugh as I ended the call.

"What happened here will never leave this room. Do you hear me?" I asked as I gripped her arm and flung her around toward the door. "It had better stay between the two of us or I will make your miserable life a living hell."

"Oh, I'm looking forward to every moment of it," Justine said with a sultry look. "But after the hearty deposit you just made, do you really want to talk to your unborn baby's mother that way?" she asked with a smirk on her face. She smiled as if the idea of her carrying my child had created some type of special bond between us.

"You will never be the mother of my children," I said, knowing there was a possibility I'd just gotten her pregnant. I pulled her down the stairs toward the front door.

"I'm ovulating," she said with a smile, once we were at the bottom of the steps. "I made sure the time was right so our odds of impregnation would be higher."

I grabbed her arm and slammed her up against a nearby wall. Holding her against the wall by her throat, I said, "I could snap your neck and have you buried underneath a fountain in my backyard tomorrow. Your family would never see you again and I would come to your funeral and grieve with them."

"Jacob, let me go," she said as her arms and legs swung wildly. She was barely able to gasp the words out. "Stop..."

"I asked you to let me go months ago. I asked you to stop and leave me alone and what did you do?"

"Jac..." she gasped as her swings got weaker.

"You attacked my fiancé and got a slap on the wrist by a fake ass judge, showed up at our dinner with your bullshit, and now this? Give me one reason I should let you go when you wouldn't give me the same courtesy."

I was nearing the zone where the consequences of my actions didn't matter. She was turning red and foam was drizzling out her mouth. All I could see was the hurt she'd caused and the problems she might cause in the future. Then, I remembered the person she used to be before she became a monster. I opened my hands and released her neck.

She went flailing around the room clutching her throat as she gasped for air. “I can’t believe you, Jacob! You never treated me like this before you met her,” she said, in between frantically sucking air into her lungs.

“I may come off as mild mannered and many have doubted whether or not I’m capable of protecting what’s mine, but I don’t think you understand the dangerous game you’re playing. The fact that I’m a good person is the only reason your life hasn’t left your body.”

She cried and murmured as I talked to her. “How could you treat me like this, Jacob?”

“Treat you like what? I’m not nearly as vile as you are. You should have never come here, Justine.” The scowl I gave her must’ve let her know I wasn’t the man she thought I was.

She ran out the front door, and I went to the window to make sure she was off my property. The street lights were back on and I saw her running down the driveway onto the street. I didn’t see a car, so I assumed she snuck into my secured community on foot.

I propped my back against the closed door and took a deep breath. Just when things were going good, there was always something. How was I going to explain this shit to Destiny?

Chapter 13

Jacob

The Weight of the World

Destiny... My sweetheart had been gone all day. I wondered if Justine had done something to her, as I took the stairs and went back into my library to get my cell phone. There were two messages from a number I didn't recognize. They were both were from Destiny saying she was at the county jail and needed me to come pick her up.

I dashed into the shower to wash up, got dressed and within twenty minutes I was out the door headed downtown. I didn't know what to expect when I got to the jailhouse. However, I was one hundred percent sure there was no way this day could get any worse.

I was livid when I found out the better half of me was sitting in the city jail, while I was unknowingly being seduced by Justine. No woman of mine should be near a police station, much less in handcuffs and detained by authorities as if she was a hardened criminal.

"Mom is going to straighten this out," I said with certainty, after Tasha explained to me what happened. It was time that I stopped playing with Mom and use the cards I was holding.

"Jacob, I don't want to talk about your mother right now," Destiny said as we walked out of the police station.

I held her close as we made our way to the car. It took everything in me not to scoop her up into my arms and squeeze her until we melded into one. I wanted to carry her to the car, as if to make sure she didn't have to stress about one more thing. "You're shivering baby, let me get my jacket out of the trunk," I said, as I started toward the trunk.

"No, I'm fine," Destiny said, holding onto my arm. She had been too upset to talk about what went down at the restaurant, so Tasha explained everything to me while we were in the police station.

From the sound of things, Mom and her friends were out of line. Although I wasn't too thrilled about Destiny's reaction, the feeling of being pushed against the wall was fresh on my mind. Mere minutes ago, I was about to go savage on Justine, and Lord knows, if she pushed me any further, I didn't know if she would survive the game she was playing.

My physical cravings betrayed Destiny, even if I wasn't aware of what I was doing. The last time I was pushed to the edge like this was in dealing with Montie. I could feel myself getting angry all over again as I flashed back to the morning I entered Grady Memorial Hospital and asked the assistant at the front desk for Destiny Baker's room number.

I was immediately met by Ms. Clara and Montie both insisting I couldn't see Destiny. They stood in the way of me being there for her at a time when she needed me the most. I knew I never should've left Destiny's side; however, Montie disrespected me in a major way, so I knocked him out cold. I bet Destiny felt the same way when my mother stood over her table talking to her the way she did.

I forgave Destiny for her ultimate betrayal of sleeping with Montie based on the likelihood of my actions leading her to react in an illogical way. But the biggest reason I forgave her was because I knew, without a shadow of a doubt, the most important part of her belonged to me. I never doubted I had her heart. I just hoped she would find it in her heart to be as lenient, if the mess Justine pulled tonight ever hit the fan.

I was standing by the car with Destiny wrapped in my jacket, holding her in my arms. I helped her into the front seat of my car and Tasha got into the backseat. I drove Tasha to pick up her car and we headed home.

"Do you want to stop and get something to eat?" I asked Destiny, once we were approaching a few restaurants.

A tear fell from her eyes as she sighed. "No, I'm not hungry."

It wasn't long before I pulled into our long, winding driveway. The garage door opened and I pulled in and put the car in park. I reached over to push her hair behind her ear. "I'm calling Mom right now and she's going to apologize to you," I said.

"No, Jacob, I'm the one that should be sorry. I let your mother bring me out of my character and I feel so stupid for doing that. I should've kept cool and walked away. After all, she is your mother and at the very least that's a reason for me to respect her."

"Mom has shown you nothing but disrespect, and I'd never ask you to respect anyone who disrespects you," I said. I could feel my entire body tense as I thought about the shady things Mom had done. "This incident has taken the disrespect to a new level."

"Yeah, but that's on both of our parts. I should not have put my hands on her. Your mother is twice my age. There is no reason we should be fighting."

"On that much I agree," I said, finally acknowledging my disappointment in her actions.

"Her being twice your age and my mother should be reason enough for her to treat you with respect, Destiny," I added blowing off fumes.

"I don't feel good about this at all. You may not feel it now, but I fear it will cause problems for us later."

I ran my fingers through my hair briefly. "Look, we've both had a long day. Right now, let's just go in the house and relax. I'll talk to Mom first thing in the morning, and what I want to see happen is an apology from her."

I got out and went around to open the door for her. I helped her out the car and followed her through the entrance, which led to the kitchen. "I owe Mrs. Turner an apology, too," Destiny said as she plopped down on the bottom stair and ran her hands up and down the sides of her dress.

"Yeah, you do. I understand how you must've felt being pushed to your limit though. It's not like this all started today."

Destiny looked as if the day had taken her through the ringer. The glow she wore when she left the house earlier was replaced with a solemn expression. Her hair was flat against her face and her makeup had faded away. "Jacob…will you sit here and hold me?" she asked, reaching for my hand.

I sat down beside her and wrapped her up in my arms. "You had a rough day. Let's go upstairs and I'll run you a hot bath so you can relax," I said as I pulled her closer to me.

"No, I just want to sit right here for a minute."

"Destiny, you can't sit around and pine over this. I won't allow it."

"How can we go forward with our relationship if my relationship with her is so horrible? After all, this is the woman who birthed you," she said.

"Do you think I don't know my mother? I do. I knew when I started dating you she wouldn't exactly be thrilled. I didn't let that deter me from what I wanted, which was you. The question is can you handle all the nuances that come with being my wife?"

I searched her eyes for a genuine answer. I had forgiven her for her betrayal with Montie. I didn't know if I could overlook her not standing strong for our love again. If she couldn't be strong for us, then we might as well throw in the towel.

"Jacob, nothing or no one will ever convince me that you're not right for me, ever again. I promise to love you forever," she said looking deep into my eyes.

"And I will love you forever," I replied, running my hand along the side of her face.

"I'm prepared not to speak to your mother ever again after what happened today. I'd hoped things could be better between us, but this is where I draw the line. I think it's best we stay away from each other."

"Understood," I said, knowing we'd allowed too many people into our relationship for one day. I had every intention on spending the rest of our evening relaxing, just the two of us. "Come with me," I said reaching for her hand.

"Where are we going?" she asked.

"To spend the night in our beautiful home loving on one another like it's supposed to be." I could see the apology lingering in her eyes as she gazed into mine. "I want you to also promise that you won't even think about what happened today for the rest of the night," I added.

"I will try."

I stopped in the middle of the stairway. "Trying is not good enough. Promise me."

"I will not think about what happened today," she assured me.

We ascended the stairs and entered our bedroom. I went into the bathroom and prepared a nice, hot bath. After lighting a few candles around the tub, I peeled Destiny's form-fitting dress away from her body and helped her into the soothing bath.

Watching her rest her head on the bath pillows and take a deep breath made me remember why I loved her so much. She was so delicate, so lovely. I took off my clothes and slid in the tub behind her. She rested her head against my chest, as we diminished our physical selves and became one in spirit. The weight of the day's troubles slowly slid away from our consciences.

Chapter 14

Clara

How Can You Deny Love?

"Oh, John, I've had such a great time with you these past few days. I simply don't know how to thank you for showing me such a good time," I said, and I must've been smiling from ear to ear. No matter how much I tried to control my affection around John, I was fighting a losing battle. My true feelings were starting to show through more and more.

"No thanks are necessary, Clara. I'm just glad to see that smile on your face again."

"Aw, thanks, well, I could repay you with a slice of my sweet potato pie. What do you say?" I said, heading toward the kitchen. "I baked a fresh one last night."

John rubbed his stomach contemplating my offer. "Woman, I'm going to gain so many pounds, if you keep rewarding me with your scrumptious desserts."

"Oh, stop fretting and come on in this kitchen and have a seat."

John sat down at the table and waited patiently for me to place a nice helping of sweet potato pie and a glass of warm milk in front of him "When did you learn how to cook so good?" he asked before taking his first bite of pie.

"My mama taught me everything she knew, so I really owe it all to her. Is it good?" I asked with a blush. After the look he gave me when he took his first bite, I already knew he was in love with the texture and sweetness of the dessert.

"Mmmmh, umph! This is delicious, Clara," he said rewarding me with another look that said he wouldn't mind doing more than eating my sweet potato pie. I looked away, careful not to entertain any thoughts about John getting me in bed. We had so much further to go before that would even be a consideration.

"Thanks," I said blushing again. I had been blushing so much around John that I seemed to be stuck on giddy. I took me some time to realize John and I spent years of our lives longing for times such as these, and I was deserving of every smile he put on my face.

"Umph, thanks to you for being such a talented cook and sharing your culinary skills with me," he said. My eyes nearly glazed over with joy as he scrapped up the last piece into his mouth a few minutes later.

"You're more than welcome, John. Do you want some more?"

"Oh, no, that was plenty," John said as he wiped the sides of his mouth with his handkerchief and stood up.

"Are you about to leave?" I asked, jumping to my feet as well.

"No I was just about to come around and give you a hug for making such good food," he said on a laugh. "But if you're ready for me to go, I could always..." he said with a raised brow and hope in his voice.

"I'm not particularly ready to be alone, just yet," I said, honestly. "I would love it if you would stay for a while longer."

"I hoped you would say that," John said.

"I was thinking we could listen to some good old jazz and talk about old times, again," I said. "I enjoyed our talk the other night."

"That would be nice. What records do you have?" he asked.

"I'm sure I have some John Coltrane I could dust off and spin," I said with a smile.

We went into the living room and I found an old Coltrane album. Of course, it needed to be wiped down before I opened my Crosley record player and blew the dust from it, as well. I gently placed the vinyl record on the player and dropped the needle on the outermost part. Soon, the sultry blend of Coltrane's *My Favorite Things* filled the room.

When I turned to look at John, his expression was serious. He was holding his hand out to me for a dance. I gave him my hand and he immediately began to waltz around the room while holding me close. I allowed the music to carry me away as I followed his lead.

With each step I traveled back a year, until I was back in 1972 kissing John for the very first time. My youthful innocence of yesteryear froze me in place as his lips inched slowly toward mine. Once his soft, tasty lips connected with mine and parted, I moaned against the gentle assault of his tongue. I remembered the moment so vividly. I fell in love with him right in that moment as time froze, and I was doing it again as we both stood in the middle of my living room, kissing ever so sweet and gently to the sounds of Coltrane.

"Clara," he said as his hand slipped low around my waist and pulled me closer to him.

"John," I replied as my hands went around his neck and eased up the nape of his neck and into his hair.

"I have something to give you," he said, as he sprinkled kisses across my lips. He kissed me long and hard against my lips once more before removing a package from his jacket. It was a medium sized envelope that he'd handwritten my name on.

"What is this?" I asked as I took the envelope from him.

"There are so many things I want to say to you that I don't have the heart to say, especially since finding out I left you with my child growing in your belly," he said as if the thought of not being there for his child pained him to no end.

"John, it was my fault for not telling you."

"Either way, it pained me to know I didn't do the right thing by you and my child back then. I just feel so blessed to be able to do the right thing now."

"What are you saying, John?" I asked as he walked over and turned down the volume on the record player.

"Read the contents of this package. I wrote them in seventy six when I was feeling the brunt of losing you. My thoughts and feelings were all over the place and I didn't know what to do, so I wrote a letter every time I felt lost. Some of them are short, but I wrote a lot."

I unraveled the tie at the top of the envelope and pulled out a stack of papers that were bound together by ribbon. "Wow, this looks like a mini novel, John."

"I had a lot on my mind," he said on a laugh.

"Well, I guess you did," I said, joining in on his laughter.

I sat down on the sofa and began reading the first page. There in vivid detail John began to chronicle everything from the moment he came to tell me he was moving away to the day he moved into his dormitory at Yale to the day he married Tammy. I read about how Tammy comforted him in a time when he was grieving the loss of our relationship. He sat silent as I read page by page. The passage on the last page read:

Nothing in my heart will let me part with the ring I bought for Clara, the woman of my dreams, my heart, and my love. Clara, I will hold on to this ring and remember your beautiful smile, your wonderful glow and the lovely way your body holds mine in place from so many miles away. I will always love you, until we meet again in body and/or spirit.

Noticing I reached the last page, John said, "And now that we've met again. I want you to wear this ring and let it signify my love for you, a love that never died."

"Oh, John," I said as he got down on bended knee. "What are you saying? What kind of ring is this, John?"

"Clara Denise Baker, this ring is a token of my love for you. Will you be my wife?"

I placed the papers and the envelope down on the coffee table. I held the ring in between my fingers, flipping it over from side to side. I thought of a young John purchasing the ring for me, only to tie it to a piece of ribbon and place it in an envelope for decades. I thought about all the tears I shed and the heartache I endured after he left me.

Then, I thought of how I pushed him away and dared him to come back and check on me. I thought about how his heart poured out in every letter. I thought about how much joy he'd brought into my life since we reconnected. The smiles we shared. The deep, burning passion. I thought about it all. Most of all I thought about one very good reason why I couldn't be his wife.

I opened my hand and held the ring out for him. "John, you already have a wife."

"I never had a helpmate or a wife. And as my divorce goes through finalization, I want you to know I'm not playing any games this time around. I'm giving you this ring right now because it feels right."

"John, this all sounds too good to be true, but..."

"No if, ands, or buts. I have people working overtime to get my divorce agreement ready to sign. As soon as you can legally become my wife, I want you to be my wife. But please know that in here," he said placing his hand over his heart. "You are already my wife."

I looked into his eyes and said, "Let's just give it some more time, John."

"Clara, this is our second chance."

"And I want to take it. I really do. I just think it's premature to step into one relationship when the first one is incomplete."

John stood up and began to pace. "If us being together is premature, what exactly have we been doing here, Clara? What's the point in all of the dates, sweet potato pie eating, and reminiscing? We need to accept what we have here because father time is ticking, and neither one of us is getting younger."

I walked toward the kitchen and stood in the doorway. I watched John pace the floor and talk about our reconnection. He had a point. We had picked up like we never stopped. He had begun to flow through my blood like a river and he was divorcing Tammy. What was I running away from?

John walked over and stood in front of me and I could feel he electricity shoot from his body to mine. And then it hit me, I was running away from this feeling of happiness. For so long, I told myself I would never find true love or happiness.

Now that love itself was floating in the air, I wasn't prepared to accept it.

"You are a strong woman. You've been strong for so long and for so many people, Clara," John digressed. "I think it's time you let me be strong for you. Let your guard down and open up to a chance to love again. Let me flow through you smooth like Coltrane, and I promise to give you all of your favorite things."

John's huge smile caused me to giggle. "You want to be like Coltrane huh? Give a girl all of her favorite things?" I flirted along with him.

"If you will take my hand Clara, there's no limit to where we'll go," he said leaning in closer to me. Once again, his hands slipped low around my waist and pulled me to him. This time, he cupped my hips and pressed me hard against his hardening body.

My arms flew around his neck and I kissed him without restraint. Any other time, I would've pushed him away, but I was tired of fighting back the undeniable feeling of passion I had any time I was near him. I let go and lived in the moment. I may not have been ready to commit to marriage, but mercy. His body next to my body was an act of nature that was hard to deny.

"I want you so bad right now," he whispered against my ear.

"John," I gasped through a moan.

"You don't understand the amount of restraint I'm using so I won't rip your clothes off where you stand, Clara."

His hot breath tickling my ear was a pure aphrodisiac. I took his hand into mine and guided it to the top button of my shirt. He peered into my eyes for confirmation and I nodded. I was tired of running from my feelings.

"Don't hurt me again," I said as I grabbed his eager hand that had already started unbuttoning my blouse.

"Never ever again," he said until he unbuttoned the last button. He had officially caught me in his web and once again.

*

I awakened to the sound of John snoring in the bed beside me at six a.m. He had one arm around my back, so I had to remove it before I was able to turn over on my back. Once I turned over, I stared at the ceiling and took a deep breath remembering the wonderful night we shared.

"John," I said, nudging him so he could wake up and go home. He didn't budge.

I sat up in bed and rubbed my eyes as my house phone began ringing. I picked it up on the third ring. It was Destiny.

"Hey, honey, what are you doing calling so early?" I asked as I slipped out of bed.

"Sorry, Mama, I know it's early. I had a bad day yesterday and I needed to talk to you."

"Baby girl, you sound sad. What's bothering you?" I asked, gripping the phone closer to my ear.

"Well, I went out to eat with Tasha yesterday and we ran into Mrs. Turner and a few of her friends," Destiny began.

"She didn't bother you, did she?"

"Of course, she started talking slick out her mouth. She was talking about me and then she started talking about you. Before I knew anything, I blacked out and hit her and then I spit on her," Destiny said as her breathing became audible on the phone.

"Take a deep breath and calm down, baby girl. If you hit her, she must've been really out of line. It takes a lot for you to snap," I said as I walked downstairs and into the kitchen. I went to the coffee pot and started brewing a pot.

"Mama, it wasn't her talking down to me that bothered me. She was talking about you, calling us animals and her friends were cackling in the background. Before I knew anything I was all over her. But that's not the worst part..."

"Oh my, what else could have happened, Destiny?"

"I got arrested."

Upon hearing of my daughter being arrested, my back became rigid. I yelled, "I know like hell that old hag didn't cause my baby to get arrested. I'm on my way to Miami now."

"Mama, you don't have to do that. It's already handled." Destiny tried to quiet my worries, but I was already too upset. I stormed back upstairs and entered my bedroom. John was sitting up on the bed on his elbows.

"Who got arrested?" he asked.

I raised a finger at John and whispered, "Destiny." Then, I told Destiny, "Give me time to get dressed and I'll be there to handle this."

"Is that Mr. Turner? And if so, what is Mr. Turner doing at your house this early in the morning?" Destiny asked.

"Who's at my house is not your concern, Destiny."

"Well Tammy having me arrested isn't your concern either, but you're on your way," Destiny said.

"Stop being a smart aleck. Are you at home now?"

"Yeah, Jacob brought me home last night. He's going to talk to his mother today about having the charges dropped."

"Destiny... Lord knows that woman is too old to be carrying on this way. She has no business running around picking fights with my child."

"Will you tell me what is going on?" John finally asked.

I put my hand over the phone and told John, "Destiny got arrested for fighting Tammy."

"Oh, Lord," John said getting out of bed and rushing into the bathroom to get dressed.

"Mama, I didn't call you so you could get hyped up. I have my own feelings I'm dealing with and I needed someone to talk to. I feel so bad for attacking her."

"Did you attack her or did you defend yourself?"

"It was a little bit of both. She talked to me like I was the scum of the earth. She didn't touch me, but her words hit so hard that before I knew anything I was on her like white on rice."

"Don't beat yourself up about it. People will take you there. But hey, after a Baker beat down, I'm sure she'll think twice before getting slick out the mouth with you again."

“I do want you to come down here and stay with me for a few days,” Destiny said. I could hear in her voice how much she needed me there.

“Sure thing. I was planning to come for Montana’s party, but I’ll fly back with John today,” I promised.

“So that was Mr. Turner I heard?”

“Goodbye, sweetheart. I’ll be there later today,” I said before hanging up the phone.

I looked at the empty space John left in the bed as I listened to the shower flowing. I thought about the consequences of our actions so many years ago. Those consequences had brought about every situation we were facing at that moment.

Chapter 15

Jacob

From Salty to Sweet

"Yes," Mom answered her phone sounding salty before I even had an opportunity to address her.

"Hey, Mom, it's Jacob."

"I know who this is. The year is 2015 and everyone has caller ID on their phone."

"Well, I'll get straight to the point. Is there a particular reason why you were disrespecting my wife yesterday?" I asked cutting to the chase.

"Oh, you called to confront me?" she asked on a gasp. "I thought you were calling to apologize for that out of control woman you intend to marry."

"She's not out of control," I began to argue but then digressed. "You know what, fuck all these games you're playing. I'm done. You are too old for me to tell you what to do and how to act. This is how this is going to go down. You have until five p.m. today to trot down to the police department and drop any and all charges you put on Destiny."

"Aha!" Mom's laugh was so loud and vicious that I held the phone away from my ear and looked at it. "You've been hanging around that harlot for so long you're starting to sound like her. Did you just curse your mother, Jacob?"

"I did and it's nothing close to the curse you've been executing over my relationship with Destiny. I'm tired of dealing with you on this, Mom. If you know what's good for you, you will go to the station and drop the charges. Then, stop playing games."

"Well, my darling son, since your respect is at an all-time low, you can forget my number and never dial it again."

"I know you paid off that judge off in Atlanta."

"You know no such thing!"

"I found the paper trail going from one of your offshore accounts directly into one of his fundraising accounts for his political campaign right around the time of that mockery of a trial."

"So what? I donate money to hundreds of people. You have nothing."

"We'll see how much of nothing it is once I buzz the ear of a higher judge that's interested in a discount on his construction site. Then, maybe I'll just call up the media and see how they will spin the story. Do you want to take that chance?"

"Your threats mean nothing to me. I raised you, Jacob. I'm not afraid of you," Mom said firmly.

"I don't want you to be afraid of me. The one thing you are afraid of though is having your reputation tarnished. It would kill you to have your face flashing in a news story about embezzling money from Turner Enterprises to pay off a judge, so your best friend's daughter could walk after almost killing a black woman." Mom remained quiet and I was sure she was envisioning the headlines with her name in them. "So I'll say it again, if you don't clear Destiny's name and I mean by the close of business today everyone from Miami to Atlanta will be talking about your bigoted, criminal behavior."

"If all you have on me is making a donation to a judge, then goodbye, Jacob. Have a nice life," Mom said, just as she was about to hang up again.

"I know it was you that was having an affair with the VP of finance, and not Justine. You were willing to let them both go down for you. Justine agreed to say it was her having an affair with him and helping him cook our financial books in exchange for your help in getting her off during the trial."

"Jacob, these are all lies!" Mom said.

"See, I wondered how it was that my mother, the woman who raised me could be so cold to someone I loved, so I did a little digging. What I found was enough to blow the lid off your high and mighty front. You've been covering your own ass – self-preservation at its finest."

"Get to the point, Jacob."

"You were willing to throw Destiny, me, Justine and anyone else under the bus, just so long as your affair with Tom remained off the radar. And all the money you had Tom stealing for you went into offshore accounts. Dad thinks the money came from your joint accounts. He has no clue that you were also stealing from the company."

"You have no proof I have done anything of the sort," Mom said, sounding like she was out of breath.

"Tom admitted it, Mom. Actually, he admitted the entire scheme to me just this morning when we met. Dad gave you anything you could ever want, more than most will see in a lifetime over. Why did you do it, Mom?"

"I didn't steal from Turner Enterprises. I don't know why Tom would make up such a horrible lie about me," Mom said sounding distraught.

"Mom, it's time to stop playing. The game is over. Toward the end of your affair, Tom suspected you would leave him high and dry, so he recorded you instructing him to deposit certain amounts of money into your offshore account," I said, remembering how mad I was when Tom played back Mom's voice over the phone. It was a good thing our meeting was over the telephone. Had I been in the same room with Tom when he revealed this, I would've gone apeshit on him. Not only had he betrayed me, Dad, and the company, my mother was at the root of his betrayal.

"Damn you, Tom," Mom said through tight lips. "Jacob, let me explain..."

"I don't want your explanation."

"At least hear me out."

"Mom, I don't want to hear anything you have to say. All I want from you is action. Go down to the station and drop the charges on Destiny. I will keep my mouth closed to the media and Dad. It's not like he needs this type of stress in his life right now either."

"Okay, I will drop the charges."

"The part that gets me the most is that you didn't care about Dad, and you obviously didn't care about Tom either. He lost his job fooling around with you."

"I wouldn't worry about Tom. I made sure he had enough money to live comfortably."

"No he doesn't. He has to pay back every dime he embezzled and, at the end of the day, money is not everything." There was silence on the line so I continued. "Why did you act so upset about Dad's feelings for Ms. Clara when you were having an affair all along?"

"Have you ever stopped to think that maybe I was having an affair because Ms. Clara has always played a role in our marriage? Even though her name was not mentioned, I could just look at your father sometimes and tell he was thinking about her. I could never seem to measure up to her."

"Mom, you have to take responsibility for being a hard person to deal with. You have to consider the possibility that you gave Dad too much time to reminisce. When you should have been all about Dad, you were trying to impress the world with your grandness."

"I'm not the type to cry on anyone's shoulders, but I had my own issues I was dealing with."

"Like?"

"Like not wanting to be married to John or tied down with a family. I would've loved to be on Broadway chasing down my next theatrical gig instead of living the lie being someone's housewife. I loved you and your father as best I could."

"Mom, it's time to do right by people starting with yourself." Mom was silent until I heard a faint sniffle. “I just have one more question,” I said.

“What?”

“Why you would steal from the company after I took over? Was it an attempt to make it seem like I was incompetent?” I asked.

“It had nothing to do with you. I wasn’t thinking about how this would affect you in your new position.”

“It most definitely affected me and I don’t appreciate it one bit. If I make this a legal issue, it will not fare well for you.”

“So your barbaric girlfriend slapping and spitting on me is just brushed under the table, because my hands are dirty?”

“Mom, you let me deal with Destiny. You get downtown within the next hour, drop the charges, and get on the phone with an apology for talking to her the way you did.”

“I will do no such thing.”

“Do it or you will be the one sleeping on a rusty cot in a crowded jail for the rest of your life. Trust me, Mom, jail is no place for a woman like you.”

“Jacob, this is blackmail.”

“I wouldn’t call it blackmail. I would call it motivation, for you to do the right thing.”

Mom blew out a gush of air and, "Fine."

I hung up the phone content the charges would be dropped within the next hour. I wasn't thrilled with my tactics. However, the bombshell Tom dropped on me that morning was enough to get Mom's attention. Come to find out, after everything went down with him losing his job and respect in the community, Tom was hurt by the way Mom distanced herself from him. Her reaction caused him to come clean about everything. Tom went into explicit detail about his affair with Mom. He also assured me that no one else in the office was involved with their scheme.

Chapter 16

Destiny

Picture Perfect

"I'm so glad you came," I said as Lynetta led Mama into the living room along with Mr. Turner. "Hello, Mr. Turner."

"Hi, Destiny, how are you, sweetheart?" Mr. Turner asked.

"I'm doing better today. Would you like something to drink?" I asked including Mama and Mr. Turner in my gaze.

"No, thanks," Mr. Turner said.

"You got any bottled water?" Mama asked.

"One bottle of water coming up," I said getting up to head to the kitchen.

"I'll get it, Ms. Destiny," Lynetta said one step ahead of me.

"Okay," I said with a smile.

Mama gave me an approving nod.

"John, do you mind if Destiny and I have a moment to talk?" she said blushing under Mr. Turner's stare.

"Of course not, honey. I'm going to check out the rest of the house and see what my son has going on here. If you need me holler," Mr. Turner said as he gave Mama a peck on the cheek.

"Okay, dear," Mama said with a big smile rushing to her cheeks to meet his lips.

Once Mr. Turner went out the patio door, I asked, "So you're just going to date my father-in-law like that?"

"I wish I could say all we were doing is dating," Mama said with a knowing grin.

I waved my hands in the air and shook my head. "Say no more! That is already too much information."

Mama laughed, and for the first time in years her laugh seemed to be coming from a light in her soul. I was so happy for her that I sat on the sofa beside her and gathered her up in my arms. "I'm happy for you, Mama. This is the love you deserve."

"Thanks, baby. For the first time in a long time, I feel good about being in a relationship."

"This is good for you. I like Mr. Turner," I admitted.

"He is really a good man. Already talking about marriage."

"Marriage?"

"Yes, he asked me to marry him."

"What did you say?"

"I told him he should come back and ask me again as soon as he divorces Tammy."

"That's a good answer," I admitted. Even though I knew Mama was giving him a hard time, she had the right to be the only one in his life before making such a huge commitment. "Do you want to marry him?" I asked.

"I do. I just want to do it the right way and, when he's ready to stand firm for what he wants this time around, he will do things the right way, too."

"All I want is for things to work out in your best interest."

"And if they do I guess we'll both have big days coming up in the near future," Mama said, raising her hand to give me a high five.

"We'll both be marrying Turner men!"

"Yep," Mama said taking a drink from her water.

"Do you know what would be neat?" I asked.

"What?"

"It would be neat if we had a double wedding." I imagined standing at the altar with Mama and Jacob on either side of me. Mama wearing white and Jacob standing there looking as handsome as ever.

"I always thought double weddings were nice," Mama said, as she gave herself a moment to envision it. "But we'll have to talk about it more after John is disconnected from that witch, which brings me to the reason why I'm here."

"Mama, let's enjoy the moment and not even go there right now."

Mama put her hand on her hip. "That's the reason I'm here, to go all the way there."

"I know I asked you to come down so I could have you in my corner as I deal with Mrs. Turner, but I don't want to talk about it anymore. Jacob is upstairs right now talking to her on the phone. I just want to forget yesterday even happened," I got up off the sofa and walked over to stand by the window. It was a bright sunny day out and I didn't want to add gloom to it discussing Mrs. Turner.

Mama rolled her eyes into the back of her head. "You go right ahead and forget about what she did, while she continues to run over you like you're a bump in the road. I'm not going forgetting anything."

"She's not going to run over me, Mama."

"That's right," Jacob said as he entered the room. "Things are about to get a heck of a lot better. Mom is on her way down to the station to drop the charges, and I expect she'll be issuing you an apology soon."

A feeling of relief rushed over me. "She's dropping the charges?" I asked.

Jacob walked over to stand in front of me. "That's what I said, babe. We can put this entire incident behind us now.

"Hi, Jacob," Mama said.

"Hello, Ms. Clara," Jacob said as he turned to give Mama a hug.

"Glad you're around here handling things. I was beginning to think I was going to have to check Tammy myself," Mama said after she hugged Jacob.

"There will be no need for any checking. Going forward, Mom will stay in her own lane and we will stay in ours."

"Look at all my favorite people standing in the same room. I need a camera," Mr. Turner said when he reentered the room.

"Hey, Dad, I didn't know you were here," Jacob said, looking to me for answers.

"Yeah, Mama and Mr. Turner flew back in from Atlanta this morning."

"Together?" Jacob asked.

Mr. Turner walked over to Mama and put his arm protectively around her waist. "Yes, we're together, Son. As a matter of fact, I asked Ms. Clara to marry me."

Jacob protectively slid his arm around my waist as well. We all stood sharing an awkward moment, until Lynetta announced that lunch was ready. "Lunch is prepared, Mr. Turner," she said.

"Thanks, Lynetta. Are you two staying for lunch?"

"Yes," Mr. Turner answered for them both. I was surprised to see that mother allowed him to answer for her, while she wore a smile that I'd never seen.

"I'm starved," I said breaking the ice that was building in the room. I pulled Jacob by the arm to the table where we all sat and bonded for hours.

Chapter 17

Montie

The Better Man

One Month Later

There I was in Miami, having flown the kids in a day early for Montana's big party Destiny had planned. She wanted to have a day to take Montana to the salon and shopping for the perfect outfit to wear to her party. In keeping with the truce we made in Atlanta, I was unbothered by the interruption in my summer vacation with the kids. Mostly.

I was welcomed with open arms by both Jacob and Destiny, once we arrived at their larger than life Italian style mansion. I would be fronting if I lied and said seeing Destiny so exhilarated, as she walked around showing off her many new possessions with Jacob's hand resting on the small of her back, didn't chip away at my ego a bit.

At one point in my life, my entire life goal was to share this type of dream with her. That was when she was my wife... when we were in love. A love I thought we'd recaptured, when we made love in our old house, while Jacob was in Miami. I had thought we were on the road to recovery. I had no clue this Jacob cat had such a stronghold on her.

I wrestled with my feelings as she bubbled over with glee maneuvering about their massive estate. My children ran from room to room excited about one thing or another, and I felt like an outsider looking in at my family.

I peered out of an expansive window to allow myself time to bite back the bitterness threatening to rise up. I knew if that bitterness made it to the surface, I was going to act an ass and I didn't want to do that. Not to my children. Not to myself.

I thought about the bright side of things: the next woman in my life would have the best of me because I learned from my past mistakes. Also, I might not have been a billionaire, but my status wasn't anything to sneeze at. I was good.

"So, man, do you want to go hang out later? I'm free to do whatever. How about I show you around the city?" Jacob asked later that evening when we were sitting out on the patio each sipping on a beer.

Destiny had just texted me to let me know she and Montana were on their way back from the mall. Junior was on the tennis court playing a game of solitary tennis.

"Nah, I'd hate to intrude on your and Destiny's evening," I said with a slight grin. "I planned to go out and hit a few hot spots up and see what I can get into," I added, while placing my bear on the glass table, which made a soft clank.

"No, no, man. You're new to my city. You have to let me show you around," said Jacob cheerfully.

"I said I'll be fine on my own."

"Cool," Jacob said throwing his hands up in neutrality. "Well, if you don't mind me making a suggestion. I suggest you check out the Lapidus Lounge. Very nice, minimal drama, and high security."

"That's probably what it's going to be then." I stood to offer Jacob a peace offering in the form of a handshake. "I'll be back for the party tomorrow at two."

"Sounds good, man," Jacob said standing to his feet, as well. "And, Montie, I've been meaning to thank you for being so understanding about Destiny moving here."

"Of course," I said, ready to end the conversation.

I needed a real drink and some real distance from my ex's perfect little world. It was hard to be happy for them, when I had no one to keep me warm at night. Except for the love of my children, who would soon be hundreds of miles away, my love life was dang near nonexistent.

"You could've caused us some problems about moving the kids so far away from their original home if you wanted to, but you didn't. I appreciate the way you handled things."

"Listen, Jacob, like I said in Atlanta, I just want to see my kids happy and I know that starts with their mother," I admitted.

"On that we can both agree," he said, sizing up my admission. "Still, I believe one good turn deserves another. So if you ever need anything, for your business or otherwise, let me know. I'm here for you."

"That's good to know," I said, doubtful the day would ever come that I would ask him for a damn thing. "Come here, Junior," I called Junior over to say my goodbyes.

"Are you about to go, Dad?"

"Yeah, your mom should be here in a minute and I'll be back tomorrow," I told him as I hugged him.

"Okay." He hugged me back before running over to the tennis court.

"Take good care of my family," I absentmindedly told Jacob as I watched Junior run and play. I didn't doubt that he cared for them after all we'd been through. I just felt compelled to say the words aloud.

"It's already done. You have my word on that," Jacob replied.

"Good then," I said before turning to walk through the house unaware of the environment. I passed the maid who then rushed ahead of me to open the front door as I left.

"Good day, Mr. Brown," the maid said.

"Good day," I said.

I took a long look around the house one final time before heading to my rental and backing out the driveway into the light traffic.

Chapter 18

Montie

Drunk in Love

I went back to my hotel and got dressed in a pair of black jeans and a gray fitted shirt. I only wanted to focus on enjoying the things available to me. My health, a thriving business, and two beautiful kids I loved beyond measure. The biggest thing I wanted to focus on was going out to a relaxing environment with good music, drinks, some sexy ladies to watch, and perhaps a good game on the screen.

An hour later, I walked through the doors of the Lapidus Lounge. I had to admit Jacob was on point in suggesting this place. The women in there were top notch and the vibe was so relaxing, it was damn near intoxicating. I walked over to the bar and placed my drink order.

"Can I get a shot of Henny?" I asked.

"Coming right up," the bartender said before turning to grab the Hennessey off the shelf.

As I was imbibing the warm, brown fluid a few minutes later, I noticed a chick a few seats down sitting alone. Out of all the women in the joint, her aura was the most attractive. She too was tossing back shots, while looking as if she had a story of loss to tell.

After thirty minutes or so of involuntarily watching each other, I decided to put us both out of our misery. I got up out of my seat and went to sit beside her. Off the top, I didn't want any problems with any random Miami dudes, so I asked, "Are you here alone?"

"It's just me against the world, baby. And now that you're here, it's just me and you," she said with a wink. She was slowly swaying her body to the music while in her seat. Her lively personality drew me in. She was immediately likable.

"Great, so I guess you won't mind if I sit down next to you?" I asked as I smoothly slid onto the barstool.

"It's a free world," she said, going back to nursing her drinking.

"Care to tell me your name?" I asked as I made myself comfortable beside her.

Her tongue lingered outside of her mouth for a few seconds after took a sip from her drink. Her plush, pink lips pouted beautifully, as if they held the seventh wonder of the world. "I'm Tracye," she finally said.

"Nice to meet you Tracye, I'm Montie," I said, turning to the bartender. "Give her one more of whatever she's drinking and I'll take a Henny and coke this time."

"Thanks for the drink, Montie. You don't look like you're from around here," she said as she swooshed her blond hair around to the other side of her face.

"Is it that obvious?"

"Yeah," she said with a laugh that I joined in on.

"Well, I'm from Atlanta. I'm here for my daughter's birthday."

"Oh, you have children?"

"Yeah, I have two children."

"Do you have any pictures of them?"

"No I don't have any pictures with me," I lied.

I did have pictures of my children in my wallet. I just wasn't about to show them to someone I just met – no matter how sexy her lips looked on her glass or how nicely her ass spread out across the barstool.

"Well, I bet they are gorgeous if they are anything like their father," she said, giving me a once over. Her golden thighs were easily accessible underneath the short skirt she was wearing.

"Thanks, you're very easy on the eyes yourself."

I finished off my second drink and called for a third. I was feeling nice and tight, so the conversation was flowing easy with Tracye. We talked for another hour as I savored my third, fourth and fifth drink. I felt so nice when I went to settle up my tab that R-Kelly's *Step In The Name of Love* flowed through my soul. I reached for Tracye and pulled her to the dance floor.

At first, she was kind of rigid. Giving her a reassuring smile, I spun her around and pulled her into my arms. She started grooving to the beat and feeling the vibe.

I was having a good ass time. The most fun I'd had since I divorced, besides that one, short-lived night when I owned every part of Destiny's body. The night that she was all mine. The way she received me had given me hope that we would be together again.

"What's wrong?" Tracye asked.

"Why do you ask?" I responded with a question.

"You stopped dancing," she said, as I stood in the middle of the dance floor in a daze.

"I guess the alcohol is catching up with me. I think I better call it a night," I told her, as I walked away from the dance floor.

"Are you sure you don't want to dance to another song? I could go put in a request for whatever you like to dance to," she said once we reached the bar. Her eyes begged for more time, while I was ready to settle up my tab and bounce.

Trayce tossed back the remainder of her drink and intertwined her fingers within mine. I had lost count of how many she'd taken back over the night. What I did know was the woman was a professional drinker, hands down.

"No, I'm good. Actually, I'm about to bounce out of here," I said, avoiding looking into her eyes. "I have a big day planned tomorrow, with my daughter's party and all."

"That's right, you told me about that. Well, I guess all good things come to an end," she said slightly raising her brow. "It was so nice meeting you."

"Same here," I said, bringing her hand that was in mine to my lips. "Thanks for entertaining me this evening. I had a good time."

"Well, if you don't mind me being forward," she began.

"Why do I have the feeling you're going to be forward, whether I mind or not."

"Because I am," she said on a laugh. "But seriously, we don't have to end the night here and now. I'm free all night, if you are."

I sized Trayce up from her curly blonde hair down to her stiletto covered feet. My dick jumped in my pants as my eyes raked over her voluptuous breasts and golden thighs.

Thirty six minutes later, we were entering my suite. It was on and popping as soon as we hit the door. She kicked off her shoes and wrestled to take her clothes off. When she yanked her bra off and her vanilla cream tits sprang toward me, my dick grew harder than a steel post.

I wasn't a fan of sex with random women, and especially one I met in a random city at a random bar, but Tracye had caught me at a time when I needed a distraction from my true feelings.

I pulled my shirt over my head and began to unbuckle my pants. By this time, she was completely naked. Her hands ran freely over her body, careful not to miss a spot. Seeing that I was just standing there looking at her in amazement of the moment, she said, "Let me help you with these."

Easing down to her knees, she unzipped my pants and took them off. I lifted my feet so she could easily slide them off. Once I was free of pants and boxers, she glided her tongue along my legs until she reached my balls. That was when she took my shaft in her hands. Her head swooped down and every inch of my shaft disappeared into her mouth.

"Ohhhh!" My head flew back and I closed my eyes, as if the act of closing them would hold this moment of ultimate delight behind my eyelids forever. My hands instantly went to her head to guide her warm mouth as it sheathed and unsheathed my rod in the most erotic of ways.

"Mmmh," she said as she slurped down my precum.

"Tracye..." I said as she made the hottest sounds that were driving me fucking crazy.

I didn't know where she learned her skills, but Tracye was the real deal. Knowing I wouldn't be able to handle her oral skills much longer without my hot seed splashing into her mouth, I backed out of her and held out my hand to help her up. Standing toe to toe, she looked up at me with the most vulnerable look in her eyes.

I reached for her face and brought her lips to mine for a kiss. We kissed so sensuously that I wanted to hold her as close as I possibly could. She jumped into my arms, wrapping her legs around my waist. With her secure in my arms, I backed up to the bed and fell down with her landing on top.

She moaned repeatedly against my lips as my tongue slid against hers. The more we kissed, the more I felt the urgent need to be inside of her. I grinded my hips sensuously against hers as I deepened the kiss.

"Condom..." she softly murmured.

I stretched to reach the nightstand and pulled out the box of condoms I bought after having drinks with Jacob. I didn't know if I would even need them, but figured it was better to be safe than sorry. I was glad I thought ahead.

After applying the condom, she rose up and, without any assistance, slid down my rod in a slow gripping motion. She began to ride me gallantly. Her wetness was slick and intoxicating, as she rocked back and forth.

"You feel so good, Montie," she said, sucking my lip up to hers without missing a stroke.

"You feel good, too," I said in between the meticulous hammering of her sweet pussy.

She crashed down onto my dick over and over again, riding me into oblivion. I was determined not to be outdone. I matched her stroke for stroke. Our bodies continuously glided against one another, until her moans intensified to the point of groans.

"Ummm..." was the last thing I said before a strong orgasm traveled through my body. "Come with me," I said using my last bit of energy to hold off and wait for her.

She tightened her grip around my shaft as she rose and fell against me like she was in a rodeo. Within minutes, my hot cum gushed into the latex. She had screamed my name and a hundred more expletives as we came in unison.

"Damn, girl, I think I love you," I teased, once she crashed down on the bed beside me.

"Don't play with me. I might take you seriously," she said on a laugh.

"Umph, you're fucking hot," I said, letting out a relaxing sigh.

Her lips found their way back to mine and her kiss was magnificent. It felt good holding her in my arms. She laid her head on my shoulder and before long we were both in a drunken sleep. I could see a trip back to Miami on the horizon.

Chapter 19

Jacob

Birthday Love

Putting on a wonderful party for our little princess was the goal. Montana was so surprised to see her favorite characters show up at her party bearing gifts. My colleagues who had young children or grandchildren all attended the party, which added up to a total of ten little ones running around playing with Doc McStuffins and her crew. The Doc did a great job of keeping the kids occupied.

The joy on Destiny's face as Montana cut her cake, opened her gifts, and mingled with the other kids was priceless. Junior was having a great time on the bouncy house with a few kids his age. Watching the joy on everyone's faces, I was confident that going forward our home would be a happy one.

Montie sat alone nursing a beer for most of the party. He was unusually distant, so I made it my business to hang out with him as much as possible. He left as soon after the cutting of the cake. He said his goodbyes to Montana and

Junior and left to meet with someone before he and the kids flew out.

My father sat at the table with Ms. Clara. They had showered our children with love all throughout the day. I walked over and sat in an extra chair at their table. "You don't mind me sitting down?" I asked.

"Of course not, you're the man of the house," Ms. Clara said.

"This sure is a nice party. The kids are having so much fun," Dad said.

"And Destiny has Montana looking as cute as a button," Ms. Clara said.

"Yeah, I'm glad everyone is having a good time," I said. "I hear congratulations are also in order for you," I said making note of their engagement.

"Destiny can't hold water," Ms. Clara said.

"Son, I just signed the divorce papers this morning and I immediately asked Clara again to accept my ring. This time she did," Dad said with a smile.

"Well, you have my blessing," I said to him. "Both of you," I added including Ms. Clara. I was excited to know Dad had snagged the one he loved.

"Since Destiny told you about the engagement, did she also tell you about our idea to do a double wedding?"

"Yeah, she actually started planning for a double wedding the first time you told her about Dad popping the question. She was confident the day would come that you two would marry," I said.

"You have a wise daughter, Clara," Dad said squeezing her hand. "She gets it from her mother," he added.

"I can't believe she already planned for this," Ms. Clara said. "Where is she anyway?"

"She's over by the bouncy house talking to some of the kids' moms," Jacob said pointing in her direction.

"We'll talk later. We have so much to prepare for in such a little time," Ms. Clara said.

"There's nothing to worry about, Clara. Everything is going to be perfect," Dad said bringing her hand to his lips.

And he was right. I only prayed that one day Mom would humble herself enough to accept all of the love she was missing out on because of her bitterness. Besides Mom, there was just one more person I had to deal with. I had to set the record straight with Justine.

My driver, Henry, had the task of following her around for the few weeks after she broke into our house. She hadn't done anything out of the ordinary. Every day, she got up and went to work and was back home by six p.m.

I had asked Henry to search her house when she was at work and was relieved when he reported seeing feminine pads in her trash can. The thought of her being pregnant with my child had been driving me crazy. I thanked Henry for coming through in the clutch like he always did. Still, even with the relief of knowing she wasn't carrying my child, I knew she had to be dealt with.

Chapter 20

Jacob

Double the Trouble

Our rehearsal dinner began immediately after we practiced our first dance. It seemed that the perfectionist wedding coordinator made us practice every move we would make. By the way Carlas conducted rehearsal, he would probably blow a gasket if I had to scratch my nose or sneeze during the ceremony.

After the stress of getting every minute detail right for two hours of rehearsal, I stood by the fountain watching my soon to be wife glide across the floor beside her mother celebrating the big day on the horizon. They looked divine as they laughed and enjoyed the evening.

Of course, I didn't want to have an average rehearsal dinner. We made it into a small party with a few invited friends. Since I had no intention of having a bachelor party, this was it for me.

I grabbed a glass of sparkling water from the drink table and was about to go cut in on Ms. Clara when I stopped in my tracks.

"So you're really going to marry her," Justine picked up a bottle of water off the table and said.

"You've got to be fucking kidding! What are you doing here, Justine?" I asked through tight lips. Justine being at this dinner would ruin the night for Destiny. I gently took her by the arm and said, "Step out in the hallway with me."

"Jacob, I am over you and Destiny. At this point, I just want to forget we ever were lovers," she said once we were in the hall.

"That would be in your best interest," I admonished.

"I finally agree with you Jacob. You found the woman you love and I'm moving on too. I apologize for all the trouble I caused you two. I'm sorry for attacking her, sorry for sneaking into your house and making the sweetest love to you. Sorry for it all. If it will give you any consolation, I want you to know I'm not pregnant so we can both go on and forget that day in your house ever happened."

"It's a good thing you aren't pregnant. I will never forget how disgusted you made me feel that day," I said with contempt. "I'll tell you what you can do with your apology. Take it and start trucking out the door and down the street with it. If you're lucky, you'll find someone far away from here who wants it. Just stay the fuck away from us!" I spoke in a low tone. It was a challenge to get my point across to her without alarming our guests.

"I'm trying to tell you that I come in peace," Justine said throwing her hands up.

"I don't want you to come in peace or war. If you keep coming around, you won't have to worry about a court system. I'm going to handle you myself. Now, I think it'd be best if you found a quick exit," I said, nudging her toward the door.

"Stop! I'm here with a date, Jacob. I'm Montie's plus one," Justine said as Montie stepped out into the hall.

"Is everything alright out here?" Montie asked.

"Everything is just fine, Montie," Justine said with a fake smile.

"I see you two have met. Tracye, you probably know of Jacob. He's the big cheese here in Miami," Montie said, jokingly patting my shoulder.

"So you told him your name was Tracye?" I asked, even though I wasn't shocked she was up to her old haphazard shenanigans.

"You two know each other?" Montie asked with a look of confusion creeping onto his face.

"Unfortunately, this is the woman that attacked Destiny. This is Justine, my ex."

"The one who put her in the hospital?" Montie asked. Every ounce of cool left him as his head whipped around to face Justine. "The fuck kind of game you been playing with me?"

"Montie, I swear I haven't been playing with you."

"The hell you haven't. You told me your name was Trayce," Montie said yanking his arm away from her when she attempted to touch him.

"I didn't tell you my real name because I was afraid you would judge me before you got to know me. But everything that's happened over the past two weeks has been real. You have to believe me."

"You know what, I don't want to hear anything you have to say. I would never knowingly bring anyone around the mother of my kids who tried to hurt her. Jacob, I meant no disrespect bringing her here," Montie said looking sad.

"That's alright Montie, man. I know you didn't mean any harm. Justine is a cold piece of work," I admitted.

"You would know better than anyone, Jacob," Justine said with high insinuation.

I wringed my hands together as a reminder of how they almost choked the life out of her the last time they touched her. "What I know is that you better get out of this reception hall."

"Montie, are you going to let him talk to me like that? I'm still your invited guest."

"You need to call a cab and get out of here, Justine." Montie waved his hand and walked off leaving Justine standing with me.

I grabbed her hand and squeezed it hard. "You heard the man. Get out of here and don't think about coming close to us again…ever. I'm not the nice guy you think I am. Do not play games with me any longer," I said, releasing her hand.

She looked at me with contempt before storming out the door. I readjusted my tie and ran my hands down the front of my jacket.

“Oh, there you are my love,” Destiny said coming out into the hallway. “It’s time for us to practice our dance.”

She looped her arm in mine and I smiled at her. “Let’s do it then,” I said before looking at the door one last time to make sure Justine was gone.

Finale

Destiny

Merger of the Hearts

I got up and left Tasha's house headed to the chapel. I was so anxious to get there and get set up in the bridal quarters that I left a couple hours early. "Are you sure you don't mind getting Junior and Montana ready? I could take them with me," I told Tasha.

"Girl, for the fifty eleventh time, I got them. You just need to worry about getting yourself ready to become Mrs. Billionaire Jacob Turner."

I smiled. "Thanks, Tasha. I don't know what I would do without you."

"That's because I'm not going to let you find out. Now, go ahead and get out of here so you can go and get all dolled up."

"Thanks so much, sis. I'm really in a good place right now."

"Hell, if I were marrying a billionaire, I'd be in a good place, too."

"No, I'm serious. The way I feel has nothing to do with money."

"I tease you, but I can see the radiance shining from you. I can see the contentment in your life. I mean, I've seen you happy before but never have I seen you smiling nonstop, even in your sleep."

"That's because I didn't know Jacob."

"Ugh... well, I just hope one day God sends me half the man that Jacob is to you."

"Girl, God will not send you half of any man. He will send you a man that is whole and who will be everything for you and your unborn children. I already see it in the cards, the day when I will be picking up the train to your dress because a man who loves you unconditionally has asked you to take his hand."

"Awe, a woman can dream," Tasha said clasping her hands together.

"And dreams come true every day. I'm living proof. A year ago, I was just going through the motions and today I'm completely alive." I could feel every nerve ending in my body dancing around with excitement. Tasha stood up, took my hand, and led me to the front door.

"Thanks for being such a great cousin and friend. I love you," she said.

"I love you too."

"Now, get out of here and get ready to walk down the aisle into your future."

"I am honored to do that with you on my side as my maid of honor," I said as I hugged her.

I left Tasha's apartment feeling so good about my life.

I drove through the streets of Miami soaking in the beautiful scenery, the sun, and the liveliness of people going about their business. In a city where hundreds of thousands of people woke up headed in different directions daily, I knew everyone was searching for peace and happiness. The kind of peace and happiness that, after all was said and done, I'd found with Jacob.

"You're marrying Miami royalty," I said aloud in the car.

I wanted someone, anyone, to pinch me if it was all a dream. I turned on the radio and listened to some rhythm and blues and within minutes I was pulling into The Beachfront Chapel. I never in my wildest dreams would've imagined having such a fairytale wedding day.

The scene outside the chapel was so natural and serene. However, the inside was absolutely fabulous. I wanted to help with the decorations and planning, but Jacob was insistent that I let the professionals handle it. After seeing the magic, Carlas made happen, I was one hundred percent satisfied.

I walked around the reception hall admiring the details of the design. The setup was more than decorating; it was exquisitely designed to fill the angelic scene with cream and beige and a splash of lime that I requested.

"Ah, look at our lady of the hour," Carlas said as he strolled over to me with a hand on his hip. "The lime colored daffodils are coming right at noon, so they will be fresh for your two o'clock on the dot wedding. Everything will be ripe and in order when the time comes, I assure you," he added.

"Carlas, you are doing a fabulous job. I don't have one complaint. As a matter of fact, I was just admiring the scenery. I can't believe this is all for me."

"And why wouldn't this be for you, hunny? You caught the eye and captured the heart of Jacob Turner. You deserve it all and then some." Carlas laughed. "Now, let me take you to see the beachfront. Prepare to be blown away," he said as he adjusted his bowtie.

Gloating as we walked out the reception hall, I looked back at the beautiful scene and tears welled in my eyes. I deserved to be happy and so did Mama. I couldn't wait until she saw how wonderfully everything was prepared for our day.

At precisely two o'clock, the wedding began. After the small wedding party walked out onto the sandy beachside, I walked down the aisle followed by Mom. We both took our places next to our grooms.

"We are gathered here in the presence of these witnesses for the purpose of joining in marriage of Destiny Baker to Jacob Turner and Clara Baker to John Turner today. We celebrate one of life's greatest moments, the joining of hearts and give recognition to the worth and beauty of love, and to add our best wishes to the words which shall unite these couples in marriage.

"If there be any among you who know of any reason why this should not be done, let them speak now or forever remain silent," the minister said.

Mama's eyes met mine briefly as we smiled happily at each other. I had chosen to wear a beige dress with a splash of lime and Mom wore a lime dress with a splash of beige. Our makeup, hair and everything was immaculate.

Then, I looked up at Jacob as he looked upon me with so much love in his eyes. I couldn't believe this day was finally upon us. After a pause, the minister began to speak.

"All being in accord…"

"Wait," a voice shouted out from the back of the sheer tent.

All eyes turned in that direction as Jacob's mother, Tammy Turner came waltzing through the aisle in a Vera Wang black dress.

"Tammy, what are you doing here?" a shocked John Turner sputtered out.

"Mom, I know you didn't come here to make a scene!" Jacob growled through his teeth. He was as shocked to see his mother waltzing through the crowd just as Mama and I were.

"I hope ain't no shit gon' to start today," Mama muttered throwing and angry glare towards Tammy. "Excuse me pastor," she said acknowledging the pastor.

"I am not here to start any trouble," Tammy spoke up as she came face to face with us in front of the church. "Destiny," she said looking at me straight in the eyes. "I haven't been fair to you and Jacob. I did everything in my power to break the two of you up. I am so sorry," she said as a tear slid down her cheek. "I know I may never be forgiven for the horrible things I have done, but I had to come here today to make amends for my behavior and I wanted to do it at this time so the whole world would know how sorry I am."

I opened my mouth to try and speak, but she held up her hand to stop me.

"I am not through. Please hear me through while I have the nerve to say these words. John," she said turning towards her ex-husband. Her voice trembled as she continued. "Please, forgive me for not loving you enough. Forgive me for cheating you out of forty years of being with the woman you truly love. One thing I did get out of our marriage that I will never regret is our wonderful son, Jacob. Our whole marriage was worth it because of him."

"Tammy, I don't know what to say," said John as he looked at his ex-wife in wonderment.

"Don't say anything, just accept my apology," Tammy said.

"Does that mean we have your blessing, Mom?" Jacob asked. I hadn't realized before that moment how important her blessing had been to him.

"Yes, you each have my blessing and so much more," she said her voice thick with tears.

I couldn't believe Tammy asked for forgiveness in front of all of these people. She must have truly had a change of heart.

"I forgive you," I said stepping to face Tammy. "I can't help but to forgive you. Your commitment created the man I love. He's a part of you. Therefore, we are connected."

Before I knew it, Tammy pulled me into her embrace and held on to me for dear life as she sobbed all over my precious wedding dress. I didn't mind her tears. I knew each of us was going to be all right, even if we had to take it one day at a time.

Once the ceremony resumed, I knew love indeed conquered all.

THE END

Author Note:

Even after finishing typing the last word, I still feel like Justine needs to get her life together. SMH. Maybe she'll get a spinoff somewhere and get it right...or maybe she left out of the rehearsal dinner crying hysterically, ran out to the curb to hail a cab, tripped over one of the bridesmaid's lost flower bouquets and stumbled in front of an 18-wheeler going full speed.

Either way, I hope you enjoyed my first stab at an interracial romance. Living with these characters for the past six months has reminded me of something I felt all along, love is love and crazy is crazy. Skin tone doesn't matter in the equation, so continue to love hard, unapologetically.

I want to thank David Weaver for helping me develop this idea and for publishing it for your reading pleasure. Special thanks to the entire TBRS & Nayberry families for their love and support of this series.

Again, thanks for reading the Breathless series. Your engagement and reviews give me – and the characters – life! So be sure to return to Amazon and tell me what you think of book 3. It might inspire my next book.

Until my pen meets your imagination again, be well.

Shani

Contact Info:

Facebook Fan page:
www.facebook.com/shanigreenedowdell

Tweet: @shaniwrites

Now, check out a fellow BWWM alpha male romance writer, Amarie Avant. All three books of the Fear series are out on Amazon now.

CPSIA information can be obtained at www.ICGtesting.com
Printed in the USA
LVOW07s2231121015

457926LV00033B/1505/P

9 781943 179060